DreamWorks Trolls

#1

"Hugs & Friends"

PAPERCUTZ™

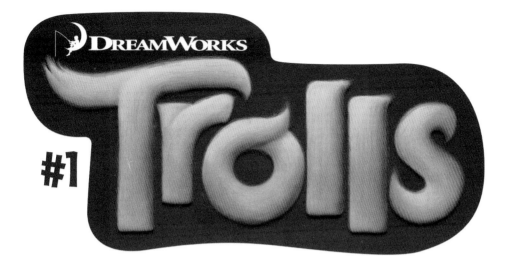

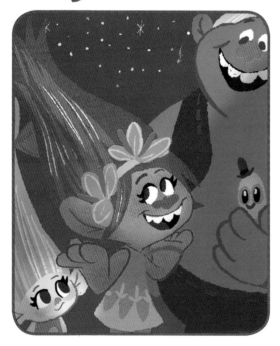

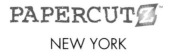

NEW YORK

MORE GREAT GRAPHIC NOVEL SERIES AVAILABLE FROM PAPERCUTZ

ANNE of GREEN BAGELS
Susan Schade
Jon Buller
PAPERCUTZ
ANNE OF GREEN BAGELS #1

Barbie
Fashion Superstar
PAPERCUTZ
BARBIE #1

Barbie
PUPPY PARTY
PAPERCUTZ
BARBIE PUPPY PARTY

TinkerBell
PAPERCUTZ
DISNEY FAIRIES #18

JOHN STEVEN GURNEY
Fuzzy Baseball
FUZZY BASEBALL

GARFIELD
APPRENTICE SORCERER
PAPERCUTZ
THE GARFIELD SHOW #6

All-new, full-color Graphic Novel
Geronimo Stilton
FIRST TO THE LAST PLACE ON EARTH!
GERONIMO STILTON #18

The Lunch Witch
PAPERCUTZ
THE LUNCH WITCH #1

MINNIE & DAISY
BEST FRIENDS FOREVER
MINNIE & DAISY #1

Nancy Drew
DIARIES
CAROLYN KEENE
PAPERCUTZ
NANCY DREW DIARIES #7

THE RED SHOES
AND OTHER TALES
METAPHROG
PAPERCUTZ
THE RED SHOES

Scarlett
Star on the Run
PAPERCUTZ
SCARLETT

The Sisters
PAPERCUTZ
THE SISTERS #1

THE WILD SMURF
PAPERCUTZ
THE SMURFS #21

Thea Stilton
THE THEA SISTERS
MYSTERY AT SEA
PAPERCUTZ
THEA STILTON #6

THE SMURFS, MINNIE & DAISY, DISNEY FAIRIES, THE GARFIELD SHOW, BARBIE and TROLLS graphic novels are available for $7.99 in paperback, and $12.99 in hardcover. GERONIMO STILTON and THEA STILTON graphic novels are available for $9.99 in hardcover only. FUZZY BASEBALL and NANCY DREW DIARIES graphic novels are available for $9.99 in paperback only. THE LUNCH WITCH, SCARLETT, and ANNE OF GREEN BAGELS graphic novels are available for $14.99 in paperback only. THE RED SHOES graphic novel is available for $12.99 in hardcover only. Available from booksellers everywhere. You can also order online from www.papercutz.com. Or call 1-800-886-1223, Monday through Friday, 9–5 EST. MC, Visa, and AmEx accepted. To order by mail, please add $4.00 for postage and handling for first book ordered, $1.00 for each additional book and make check payable to NBM Publishing. Send to: Papercutz, 160 Broadway, Suite 700, East Wing, New York, NY 10038.

THE SMURFS, THE GARFIELD SHOW, BARBIE, TROLLS, GERONIMO STILTON, THEA STILTON, FUZZY BASEBALL, THE LUNCH WITCH, NANCY DREW DIARIES, THE RED SHOES, ANNE OF GREEN BAGELS, and SCARLETT graphic novels are also available wherever e-books are sold.

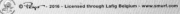

DreamWorks

Trolls

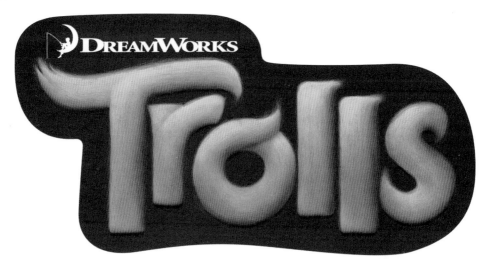

TABLE OF CONTENTS

"Hugs & Friends"

Dave Scheidt – Trolls Writer
Tini Howard – Bergens Writer
Kathryn Hudson – Artist and Colorist
Tom Orzechowski – Letterer

Dawn Guzzo – Design/Production
Rachel Pinnelas – Production Coordinator
Bethany Bryan – Editor
Jeff Whitman – Assistant Managing Editor
Jim Salicrup
Editor-in-Chief

ISBN: 978-1-62991-583-8 paperback edition
ISBN: 978-1-62991-584-5 hardcover edition

Papercutz books may be purchased for business or promotional use.
For information on bulk purchases please contact Macmillan Corporate and
Premium Sales Department at (800) 221-7945 x5442.

Printed in Canada
September 2016 by Marquis

Distributed by Macmillan
First Printing

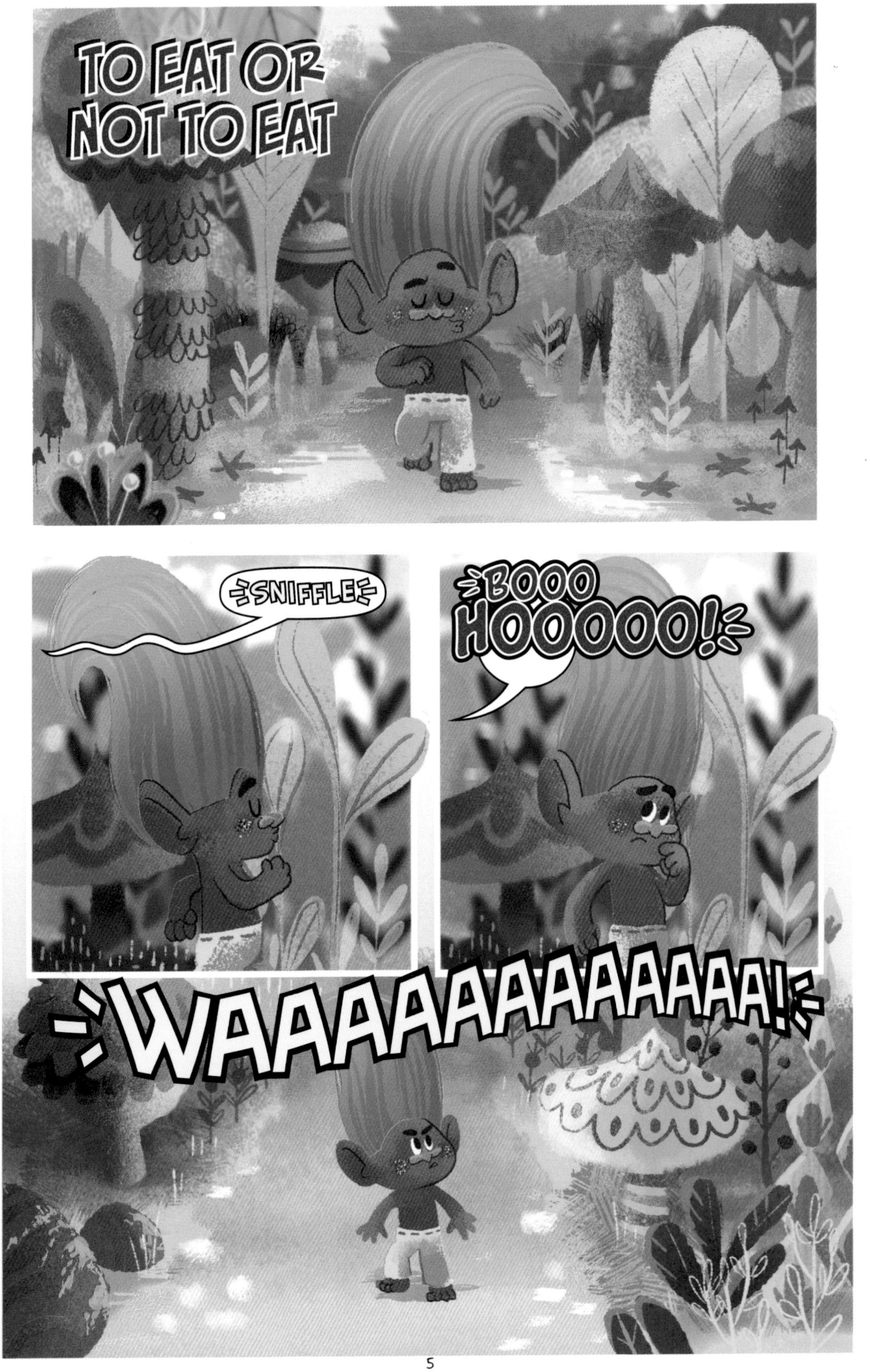

TO EAT OR NOT TO EAT
SNIFFLE
BOOO HOOOOOO!
WAAAAAAAAAAAAAA!

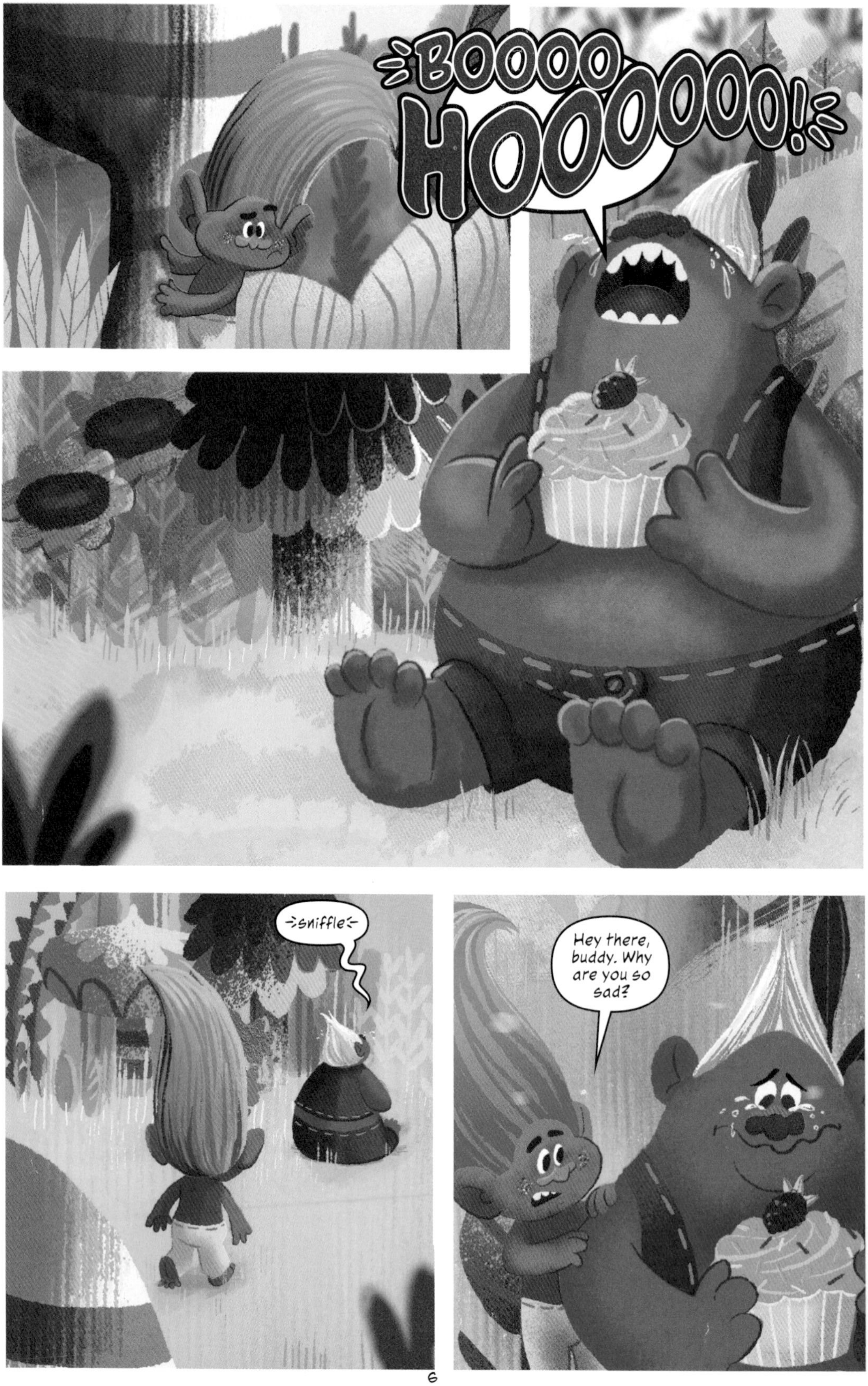
BOOOO HOOOOOOO!
sniffle
Hey there, buddy. Why are you so sad?

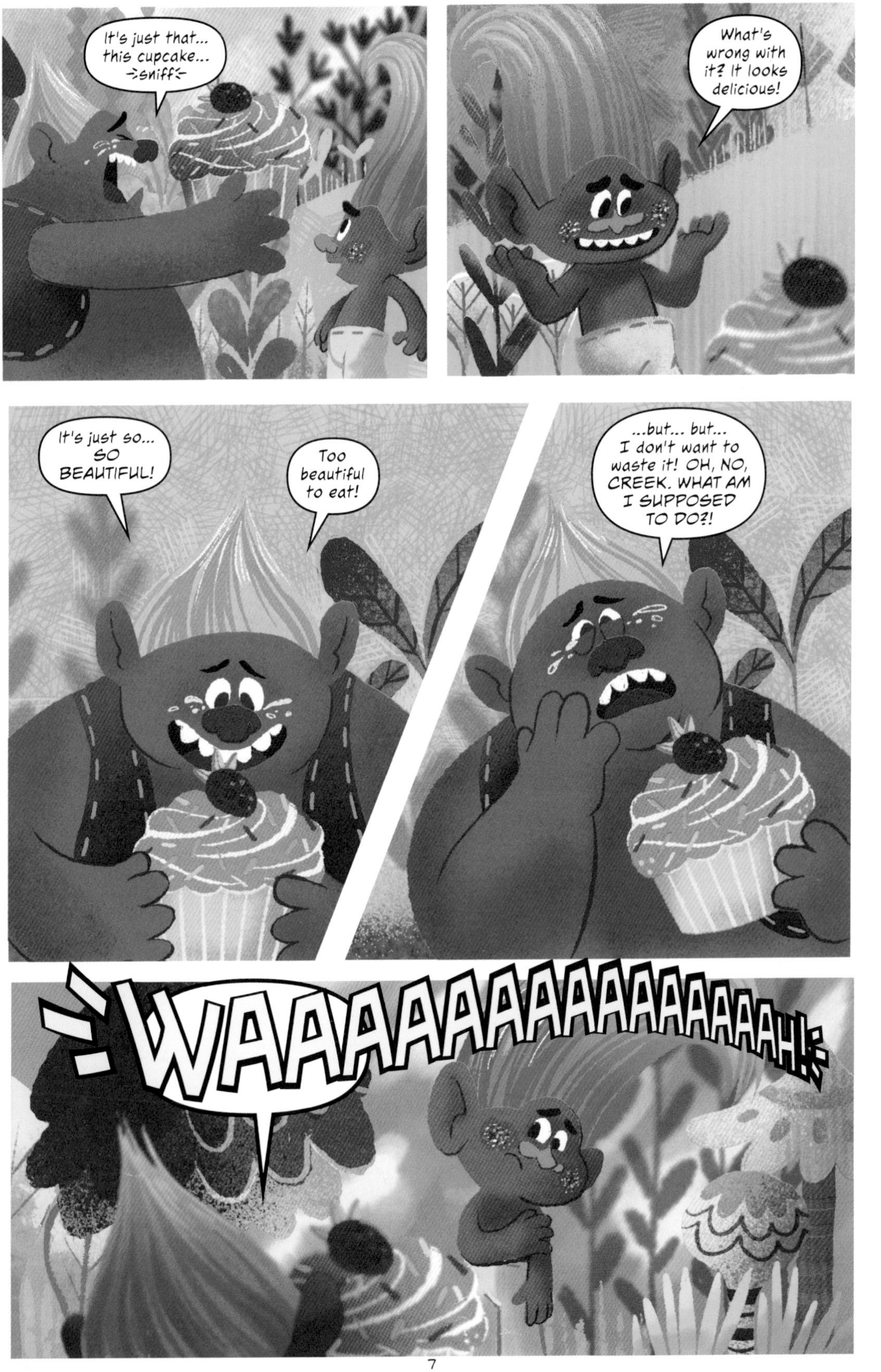
It's just that... this cupcake... -sniff-
What's wrong with it? It looks delicious!
It's just so... SO BEAUTIFUL!
Too beautiful to eat!
...but... but... I don't want to waste it! OH, NO, CREEK. WHAT AM I SUPPOSED TO DO?!
WAAAAAAAAAAAAAAAH!!

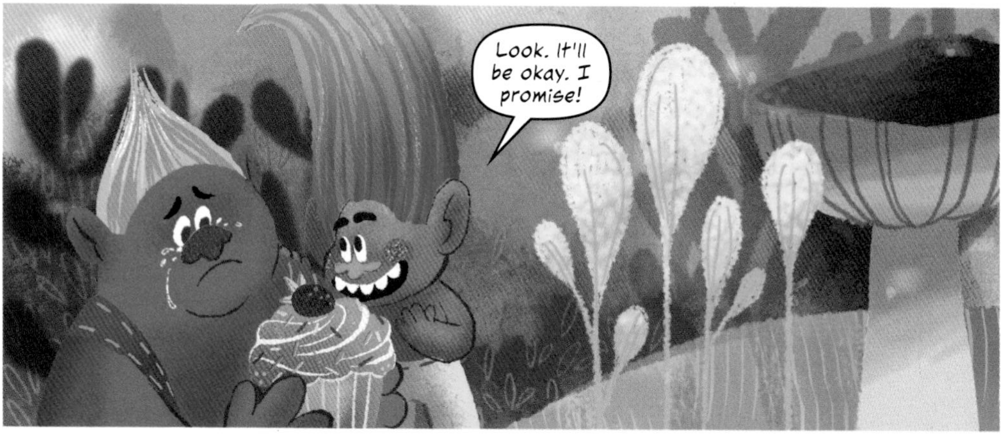
Look. It'll be okay. I promise!

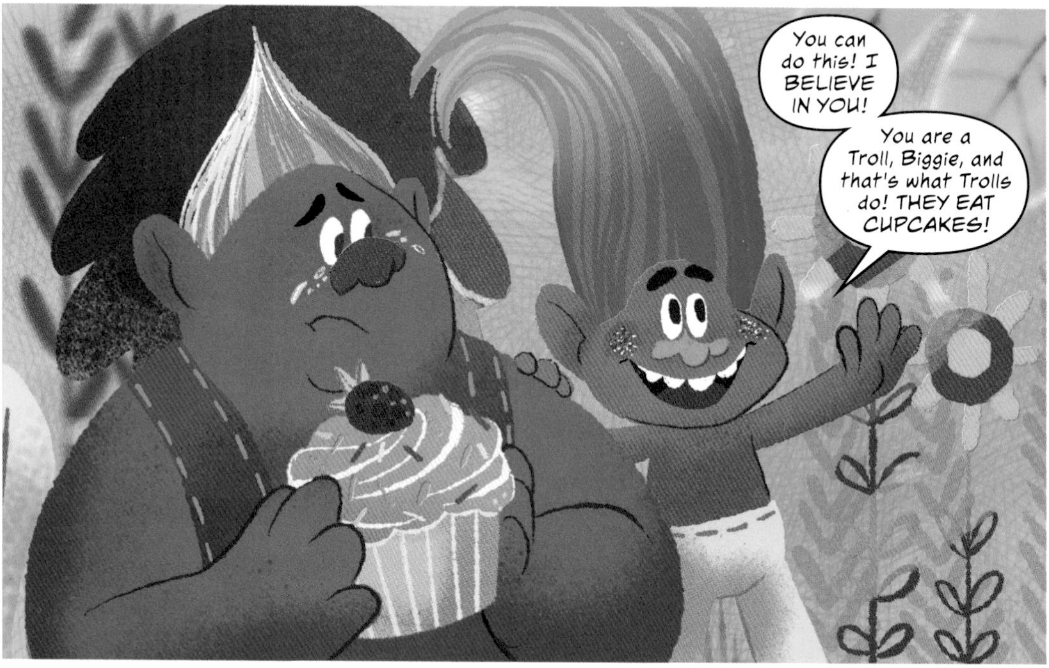
You can do this! I BELIEVE IN YOU!
You are a Troll, Biggie, and that's what Trolls do! THEY EAT CUPCAKES!

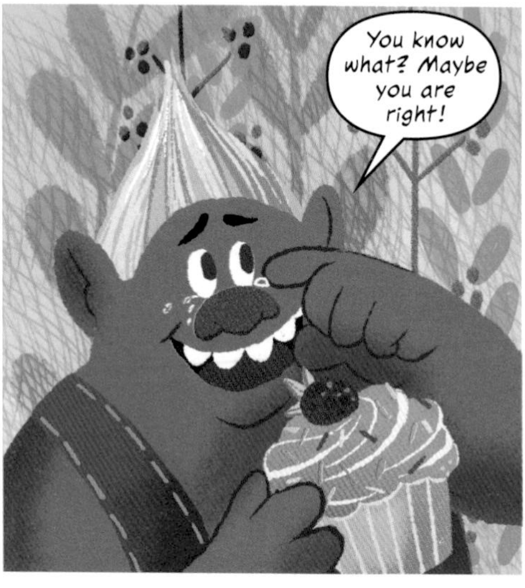
You know what? Maybe you are right!

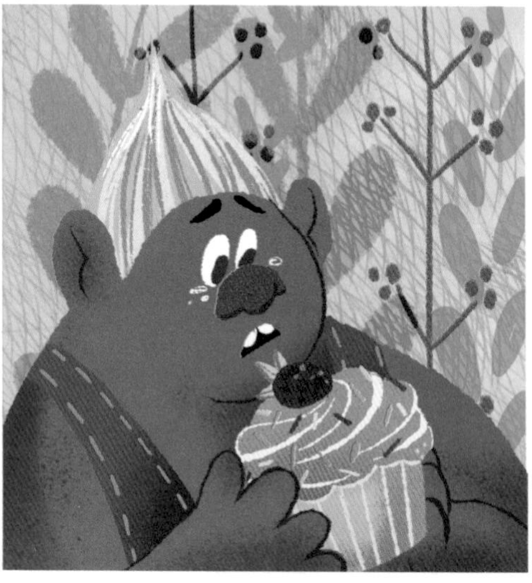

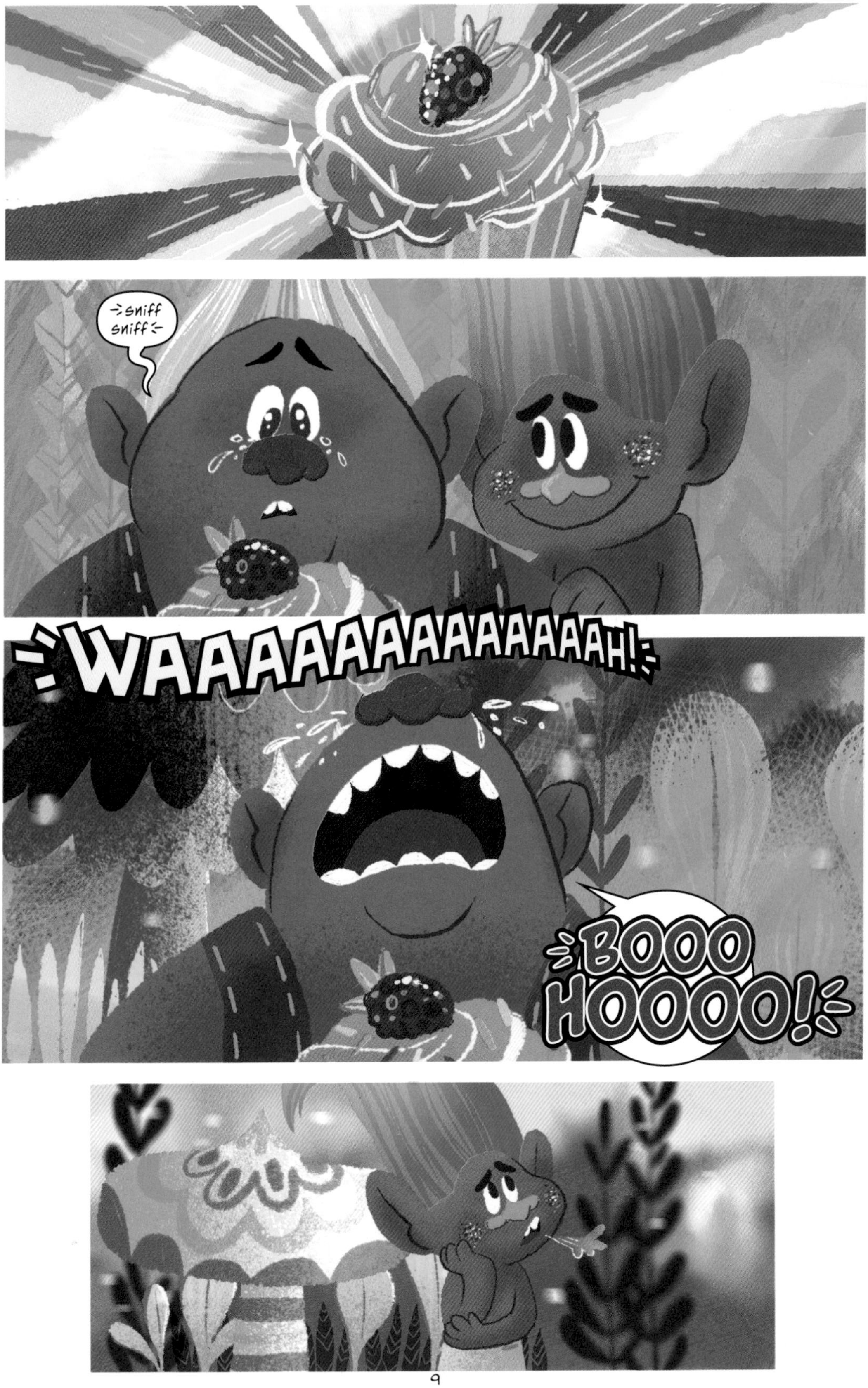

sniff sniff
WAAAAAAAAAAAAAH!
BOOO HOOOO!

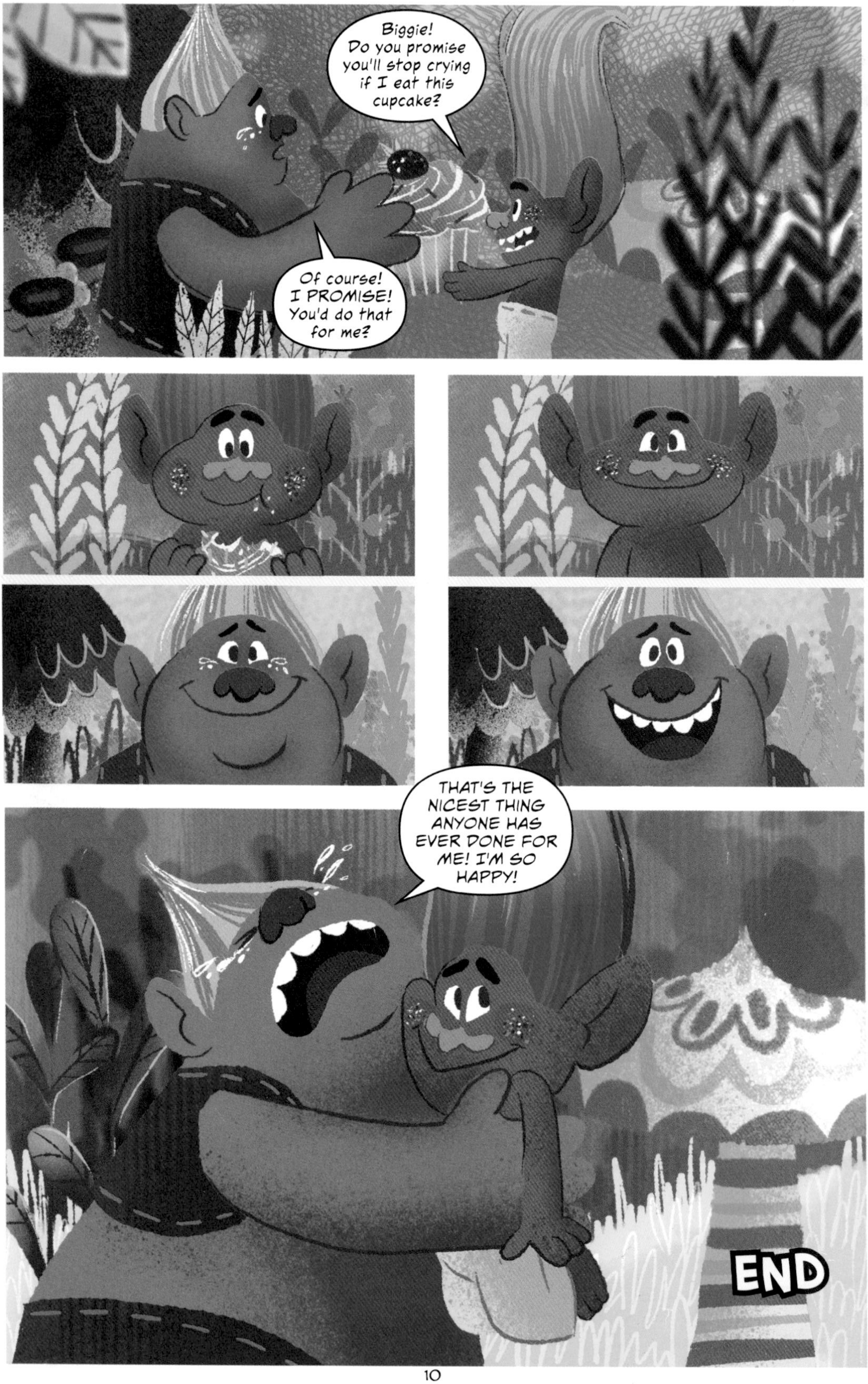
Biggie! Do you promise you'll stop crying if I eat this cupcake?
Of course! I PROMISE! You'd do that for me?
THAT'S THE NICEST THING ANYONE HAS EVER DONE FOR ME! I'M SO HAPPY!
END

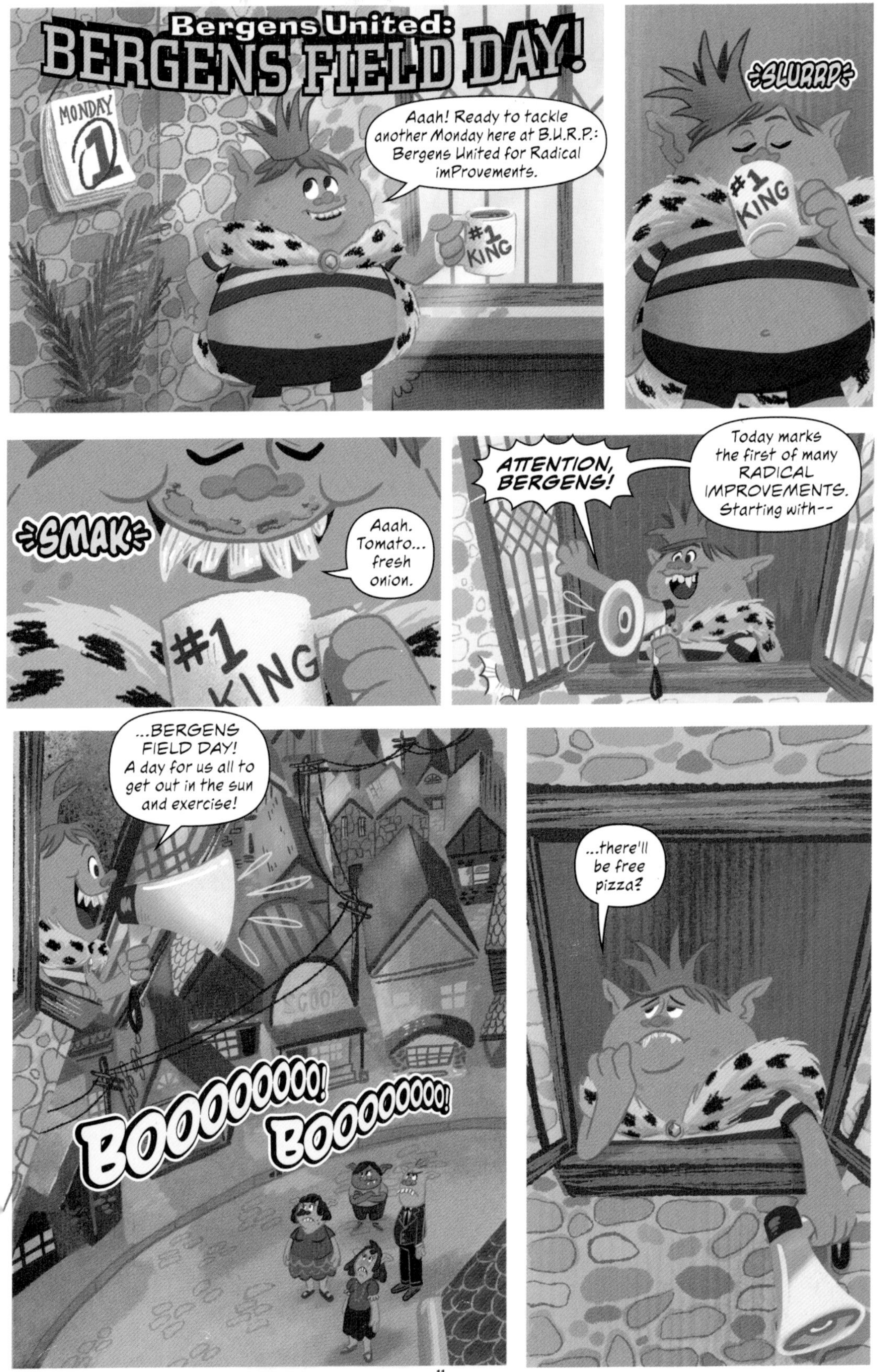
Bergens United:
BERGENS FIELD DAY!
MONDAY
1
Aaah! Ready to tackle another Monday here at B.U.R.P.: Bergens United for Radical imProvements.
#1 KING
SLURRP
#1 KING
SMAK
Aaah. Tomato... fresh onion.
#1 KING
ATTENTION, BERGENS!
Today marks the first of many RADICAL IMPROVEMENTS. Starting with--
...BERGENS FIELD DAY! A day for us all to get out in the sun and exercise!
SCOOP
BOOOOOOOO! BOOOOOOOO!
...there'll be free pizza?

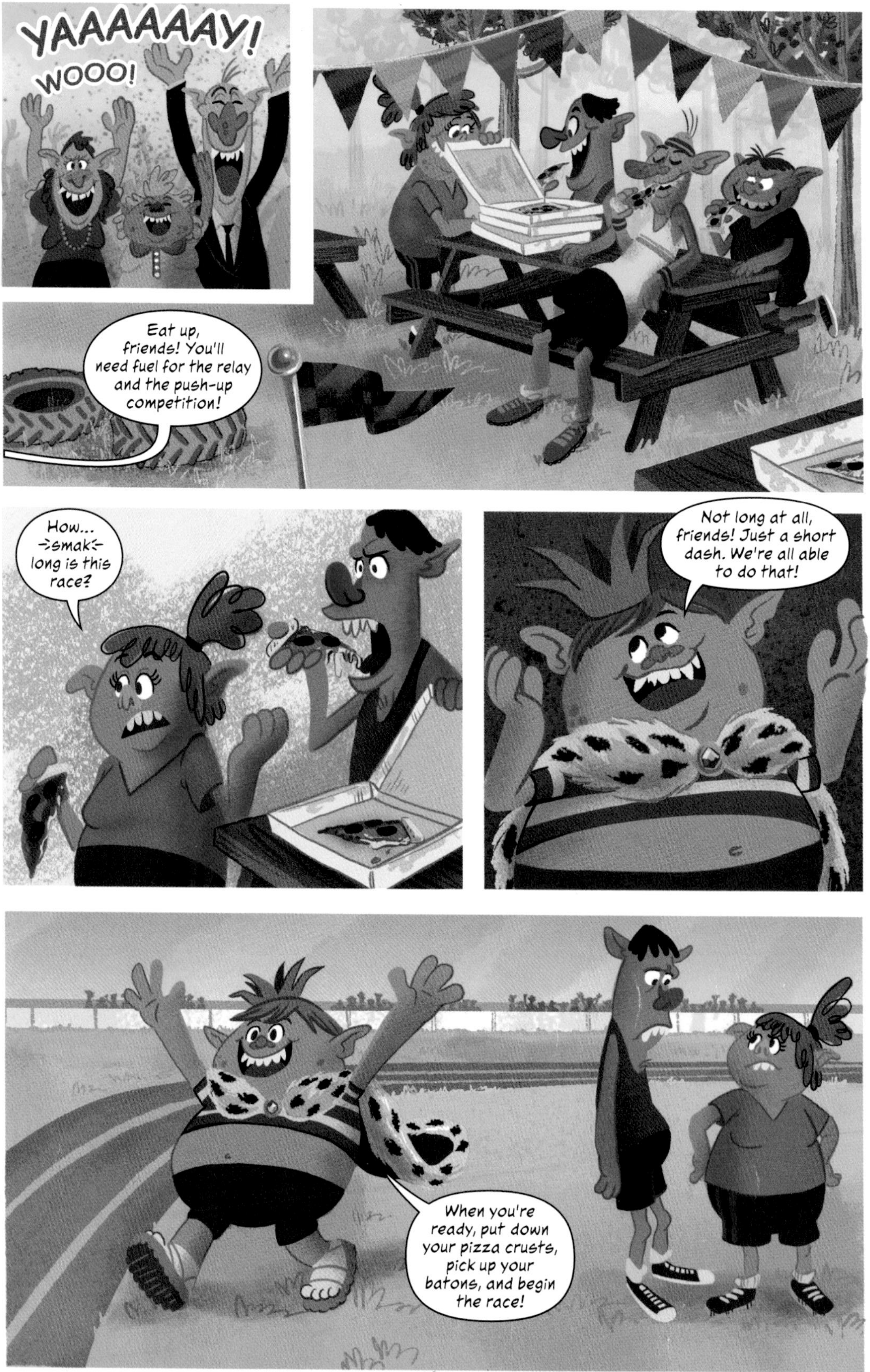
YAAAAAAY!
WOOO!
Eat up, friends! You'll need fuel for the relay and the push-up competition!
How... ->smak<- long is this race?
Not long at all, friends! Just a short dash. We're all able to do that!
When you're ready, put down your pizza crusts, pick up your batons, and begin the race!

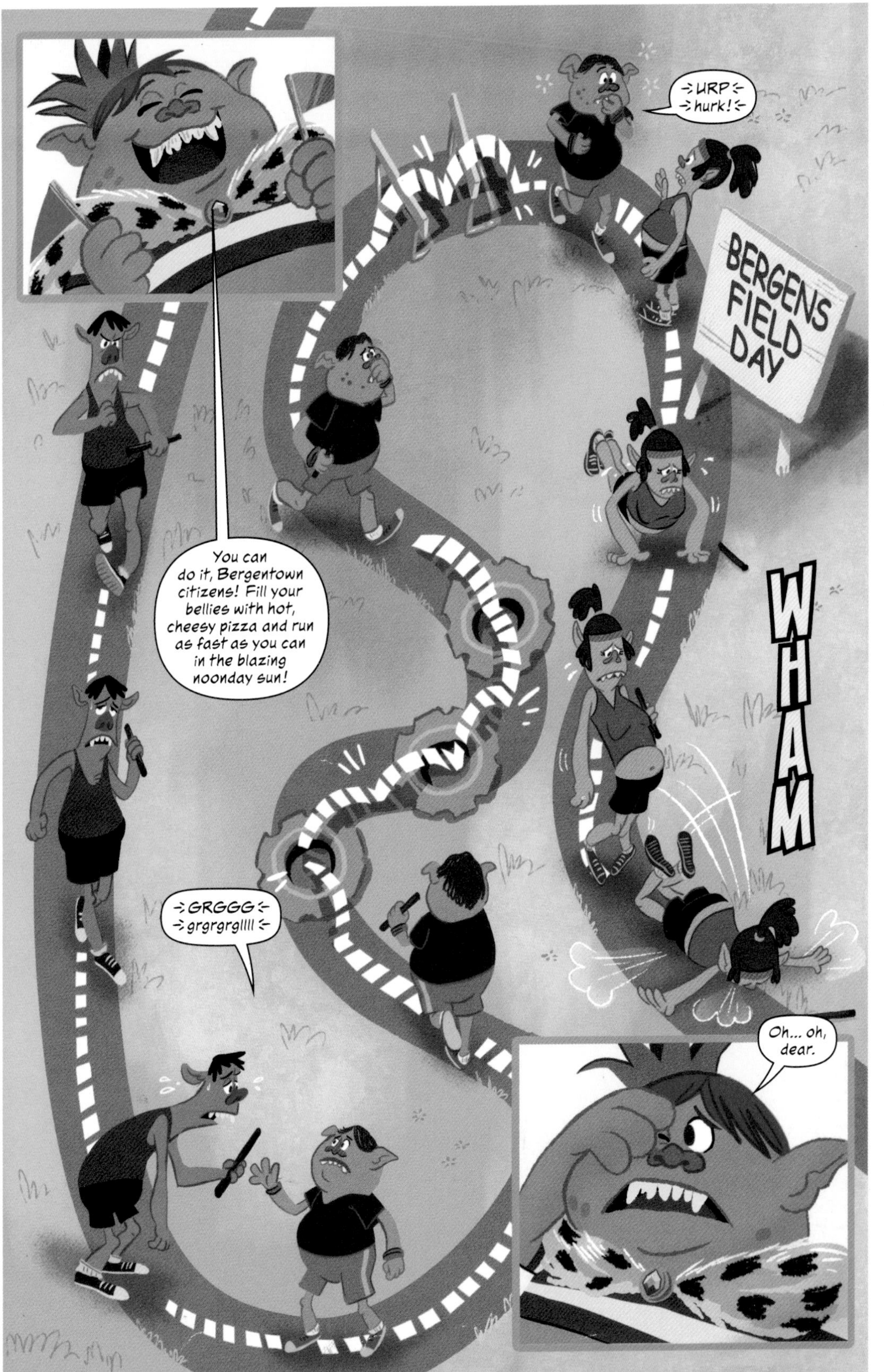
You can do it, Bergentown citizens! Fill your bellies with hot, cheesy pizza and run as fast as you can in the blazing noonday sun!
URP hurk!
BERGENS FIELD DAY
WHAM
GRGGG grgrgrglll
Oh... oh, dear.

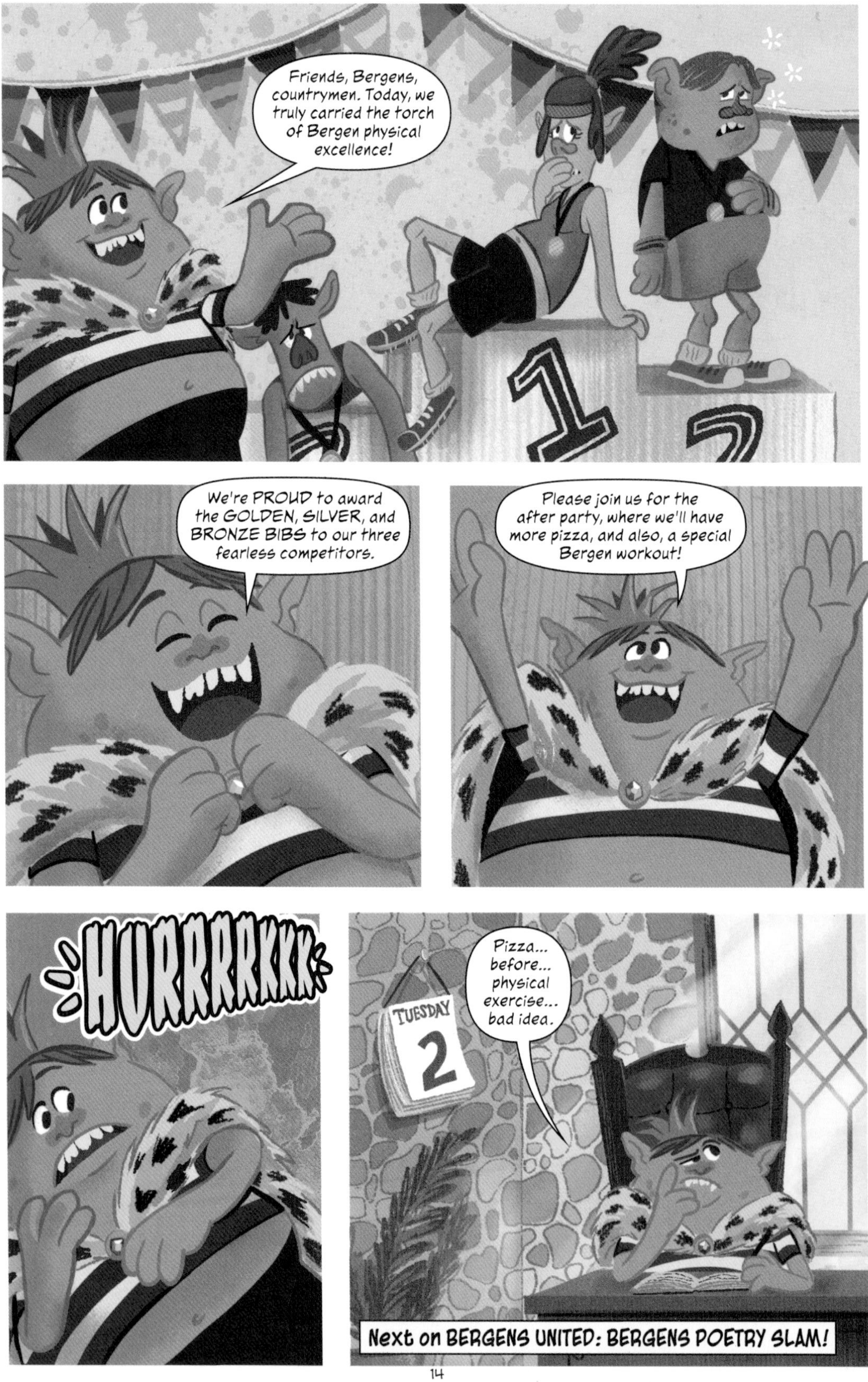

Friends, Bergens, countrymen. Today, we truly carried the torch of Bergen physical excellence!
We're PROUD to award the GOLDEN, SILVER, and BRONZE BIBS to our three fearless competitors.
Please join us for the after party, where we'll have more pizza, and also, a special Bergen workout!
HURRRRKKK
TUESDAY
2
Pizza... before... physical exercise... bad idea.
Next on BERGENS UNITED: BERGENS POETRY SLAM!

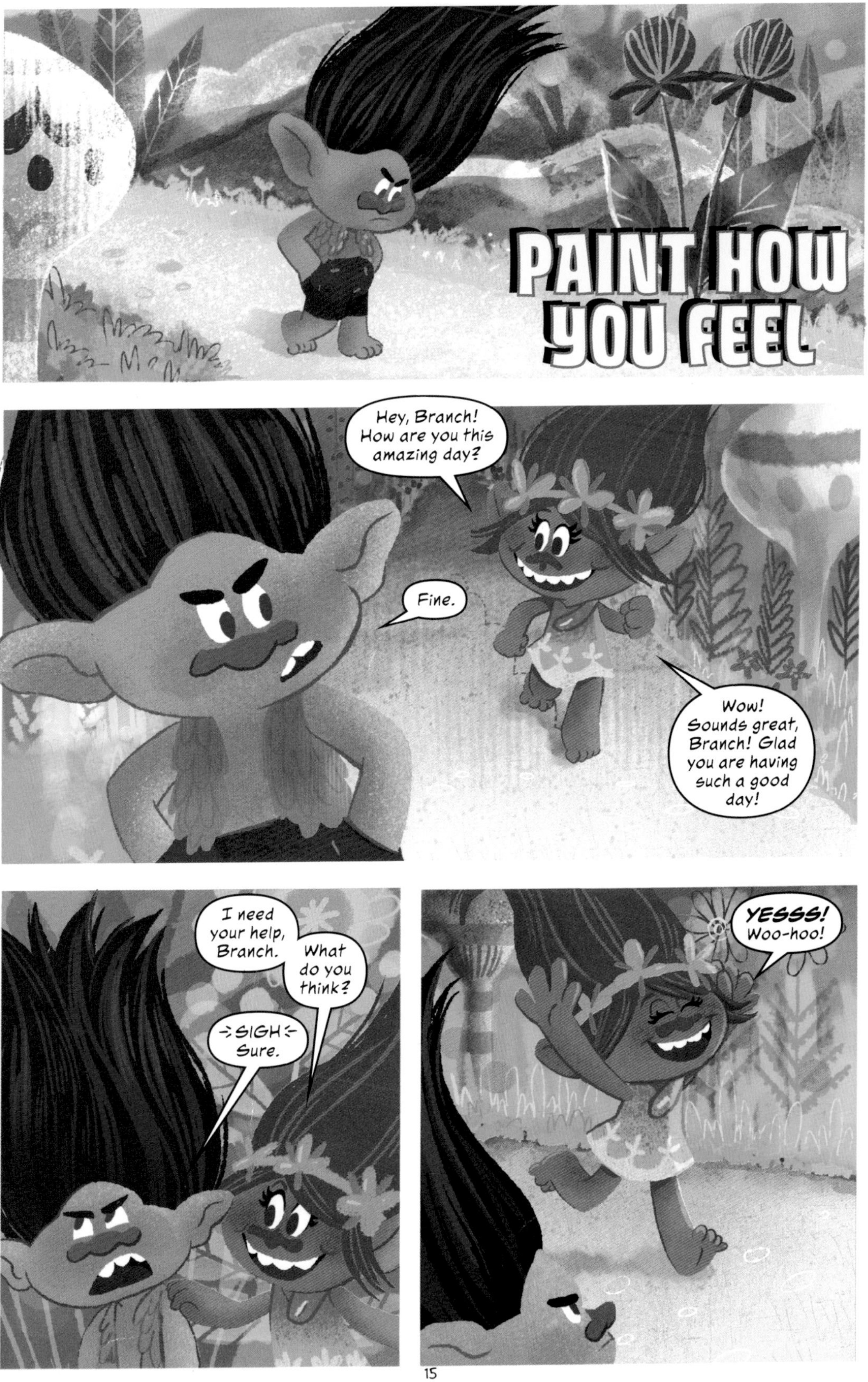
PAINT HOW YOU FEEL
Hey, Branch! How are you this amazing day?
Fine.
Wow! Sounds great, Branch! Glad you are having such a good day!
I need your help, Branch.
What do you think?
SIGH Sure.
YESSS! Woo-hoo!

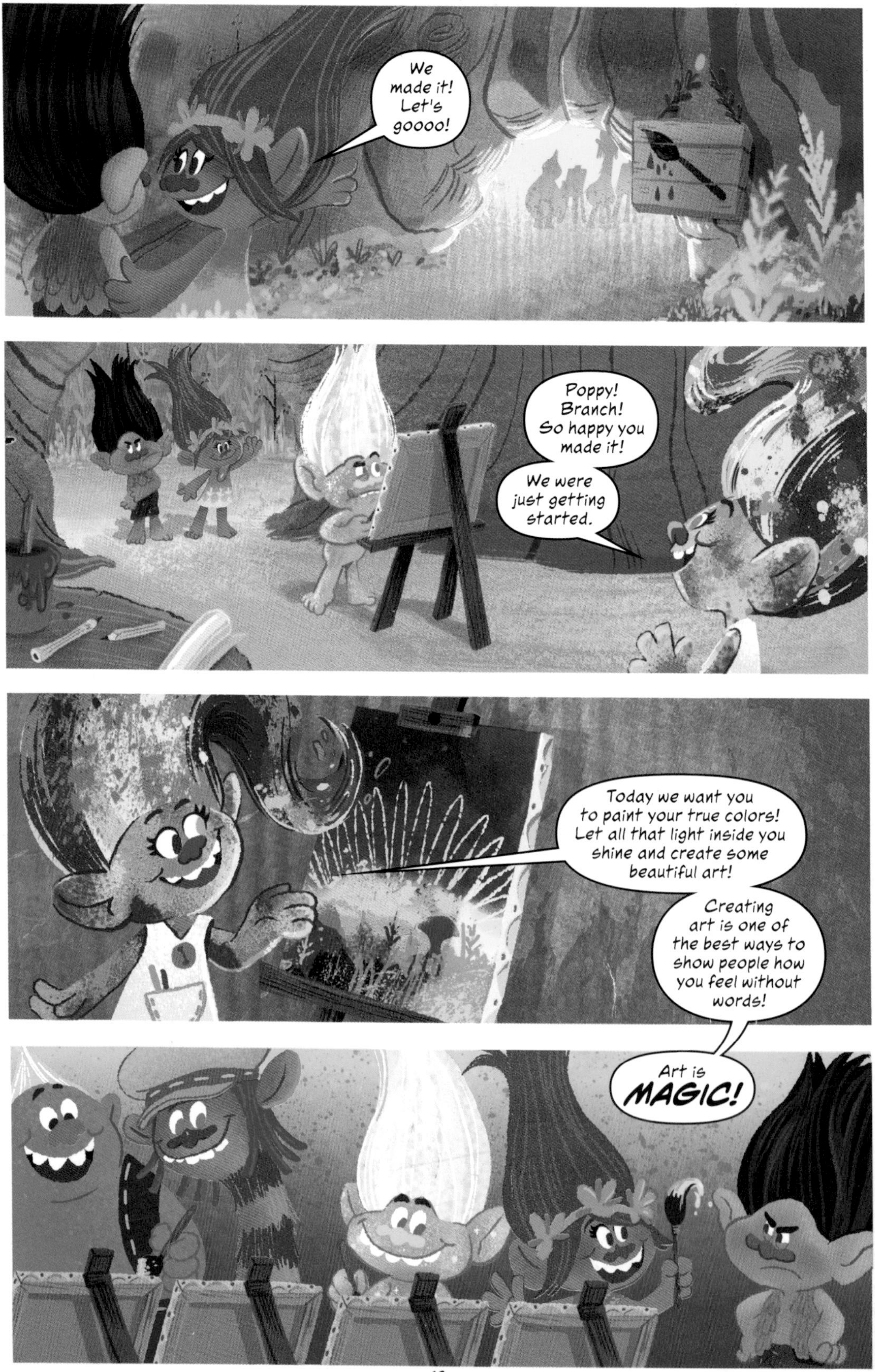

We made it! Let's goooo!
Poppy! Branch! So happy you made it!
We were just getting started.
Today we want you to paint your true colors! Let all that light inside you shine and create some beautiful art!
Creating art is one of the best ways to show people how you feel without words!
Art is MAGIC!

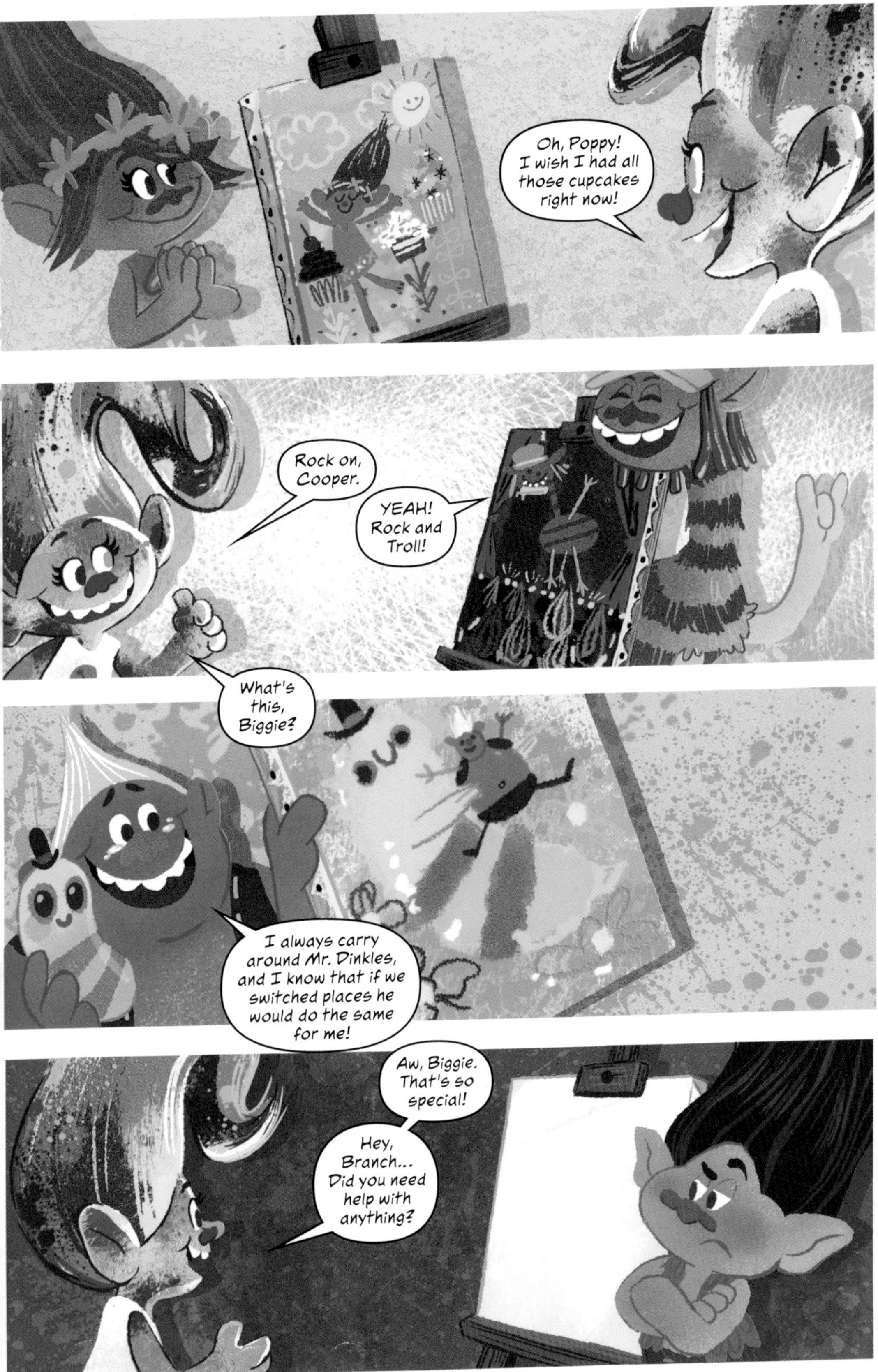
Oh, Poppy! I wish I had all those cupcakes right now!
Rock on, Cooper.
YEAH! Rock and Troll!
What's this, Biggie?
I always carry around Mr. Dinkles, and I know that if we switched places he would do the same for me!
Aw, Biggie. That's so special!
Hey, Branch... Did you need help with anything?

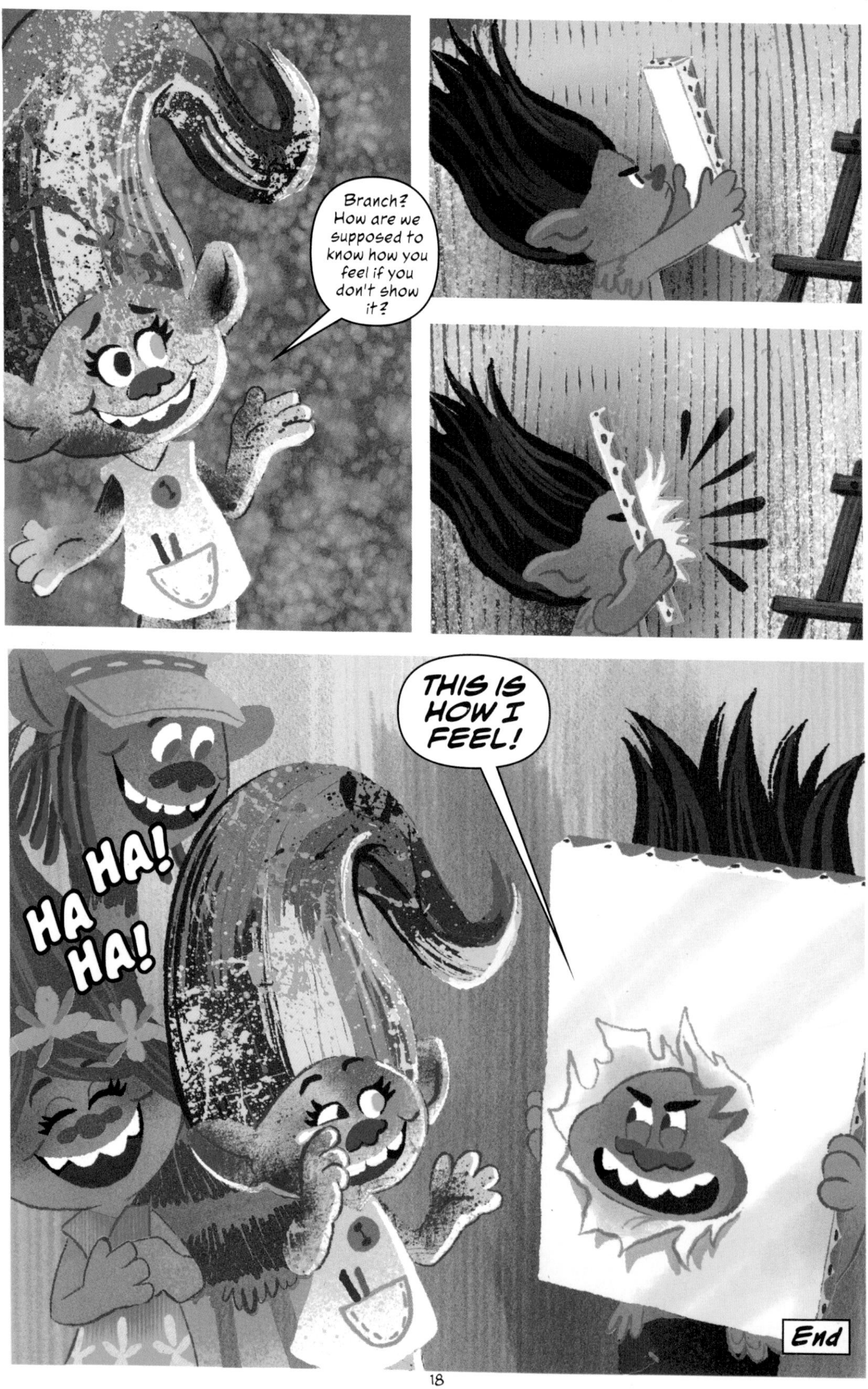
Branch? How are we supposed to know how you feel if you don't show it?
THIS IS HOW I FEEL!
HA HA! HA HA!
End

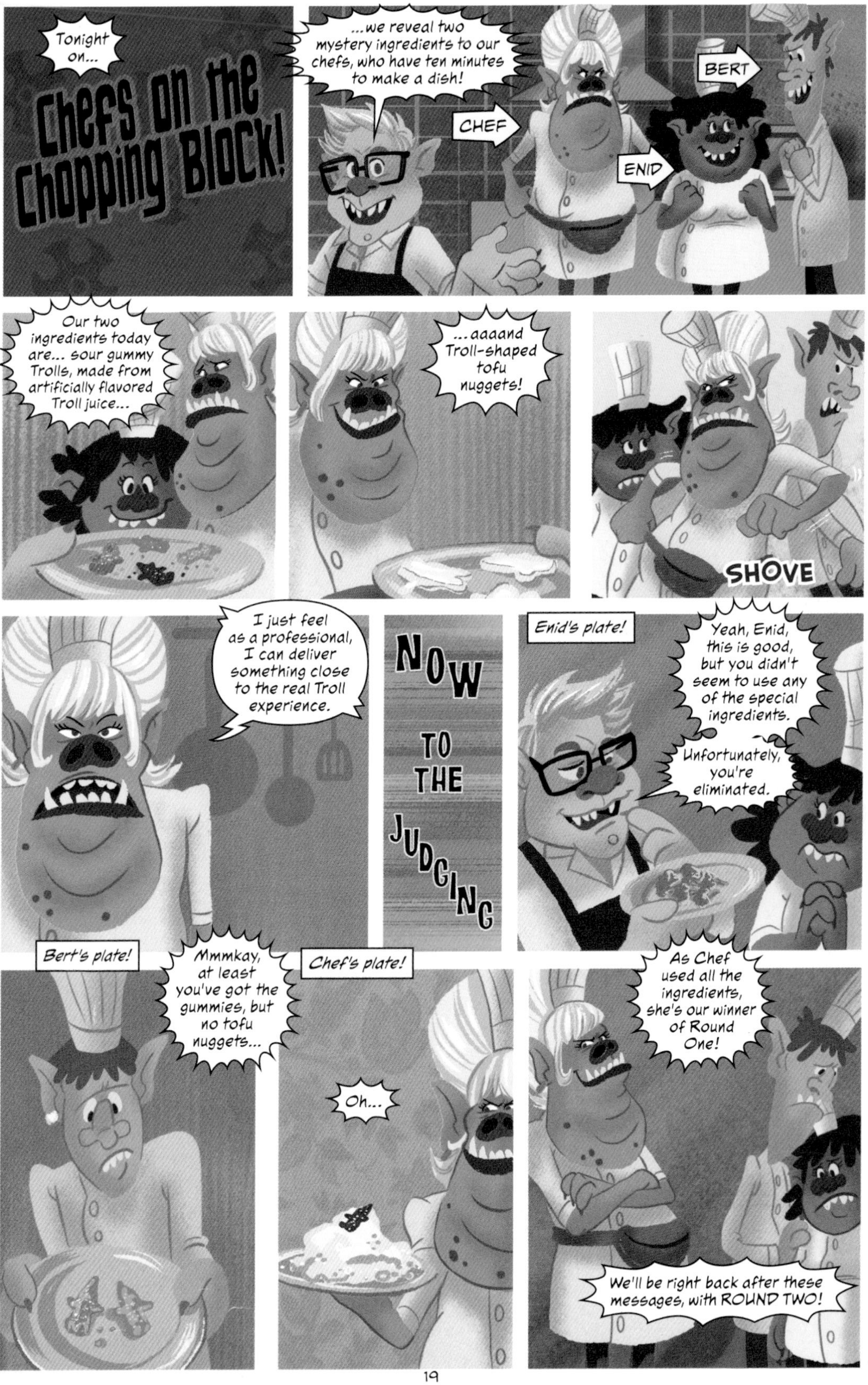
Tonight on...
Chefs on the Chopping Block!
...we reveal two mystery ingredients to our chefs, who have ten minutes to make a dish!
CHEF
BERT
ENID
Our two ingredients today are... sour gummy Trolls, made from artificially flavored Troll juice...
...aaaand Troll-shaped tofu nuggets!
SHOVE
I just feel as a professional, I can deliver something close to the real Troll experience.
NOW TO THE JUDGING
Enid's plate!
Yeah, Enid, this is good, but you didn't seem to use any of the special ingredients.
Unfortunately, you're eliminated.
Bert's plate!
Mmmkay, at least you've got the gummies, but no tofu nuggets...
Chef's plate!
Oh...
As Chef used all the ingredients, she's our winner of Round One!
We'll be right back after these messages, with ROUND TWO!

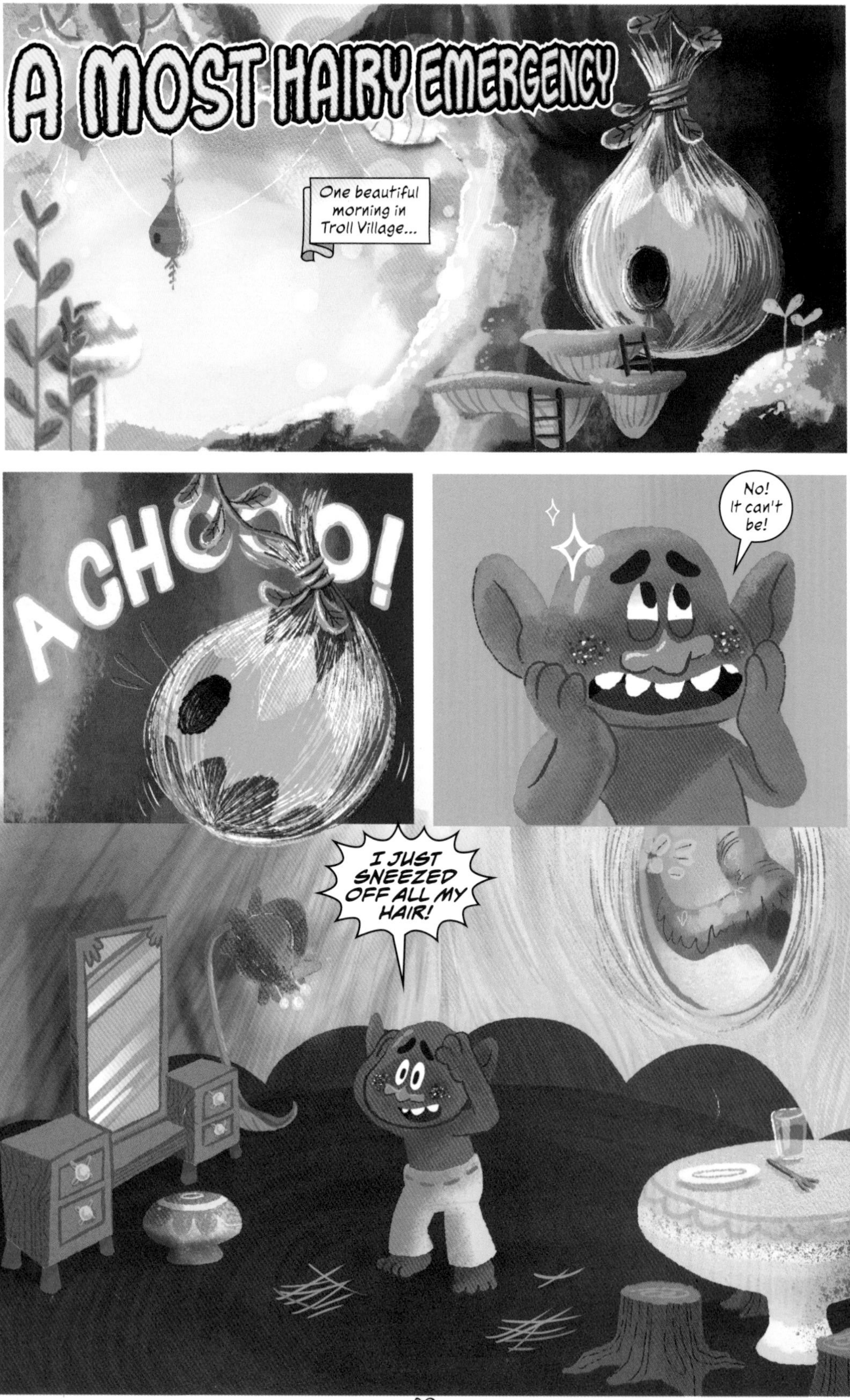
A MOST HAIRY EMERGENCY
One beautiful morning in Troll Village...
No! It can't be!
I JUST SNEEZED OFF ALL MY HAIR!

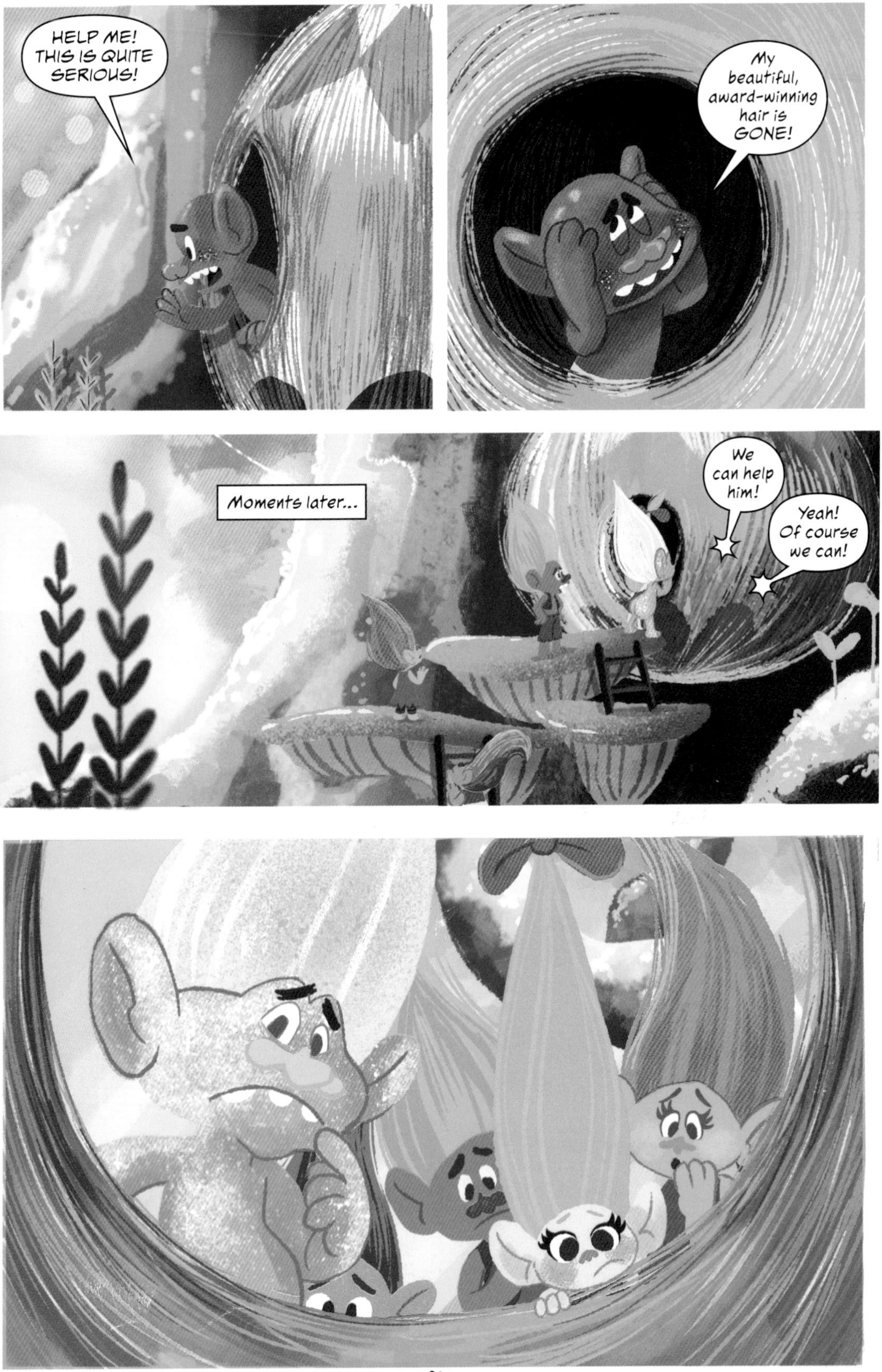
HELP ME! THIS IS QUITE SERIOUS!
My beautiful, award-winning hair is GONE!
Moments later...
We can help him!
Yeah! Of course we can!

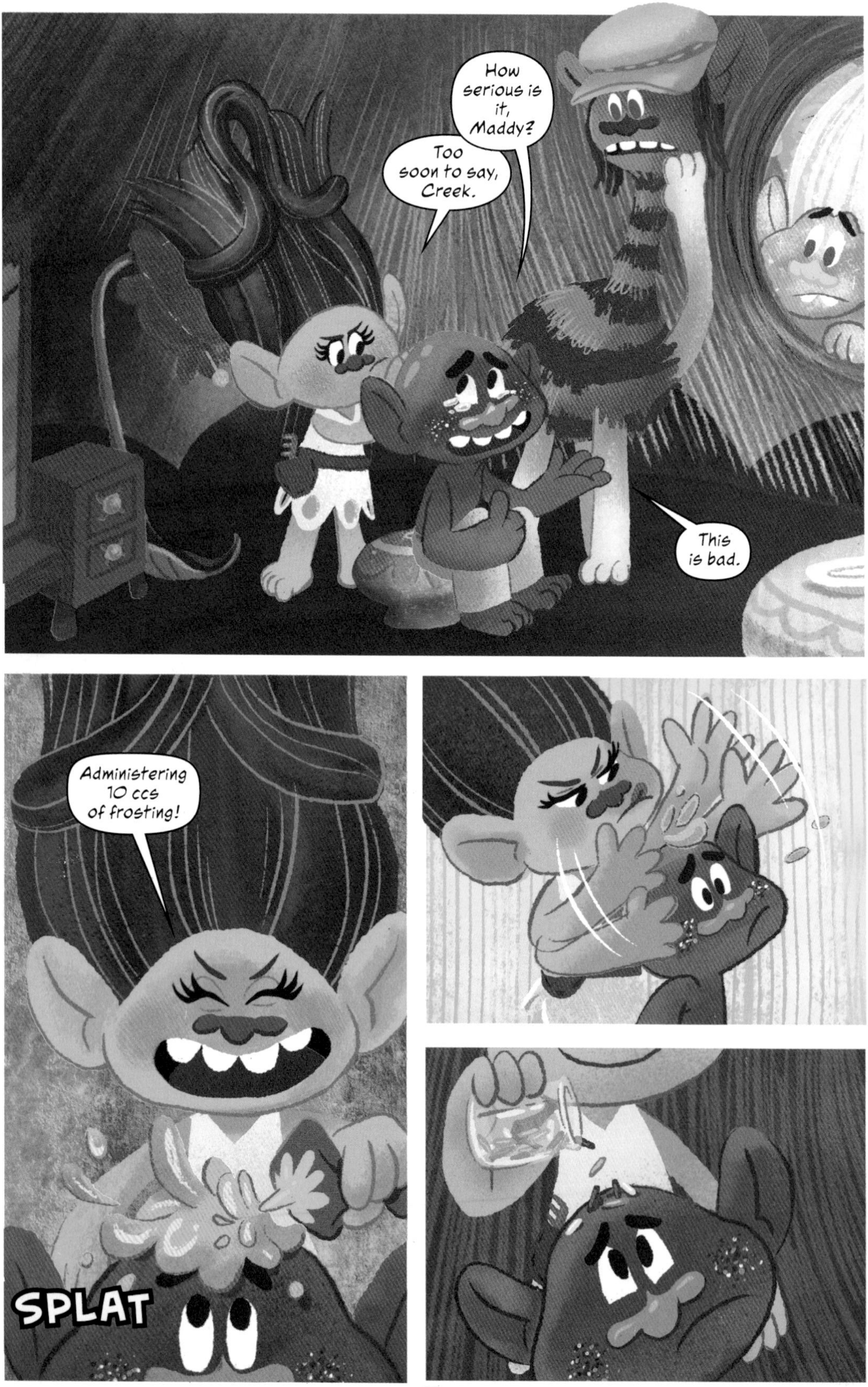
How serious is it, Maddy?
Too soon to say, Creek.
This is bad.
Administering 10 ccs of frosting!
SPLAT

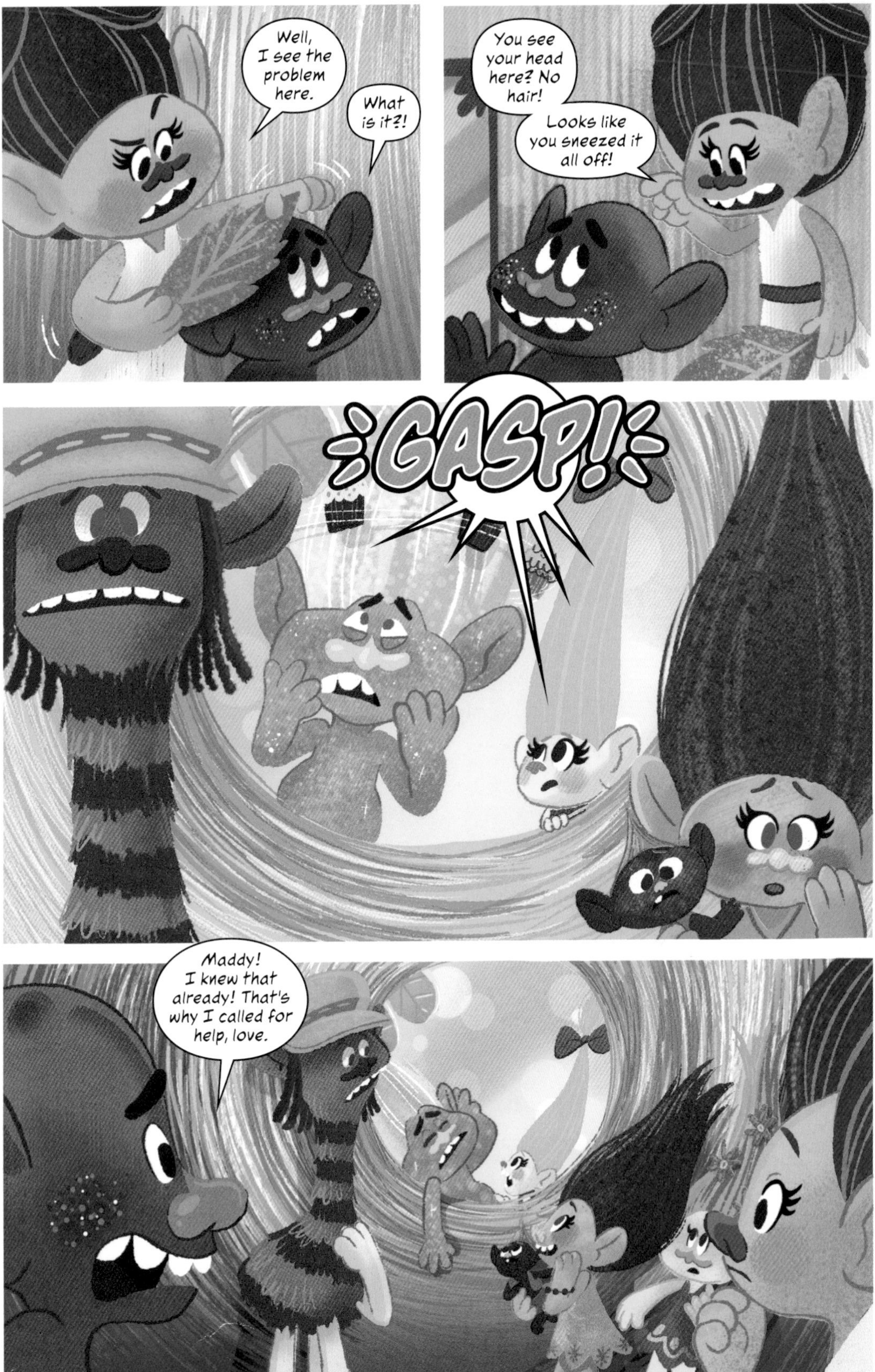
Well, I see the problem here.
What is it?!
You see your head here? No hair!
Looks like you sneezed it all off!
GASP!
Maddy! I knew that already! That's why I called for help, love.

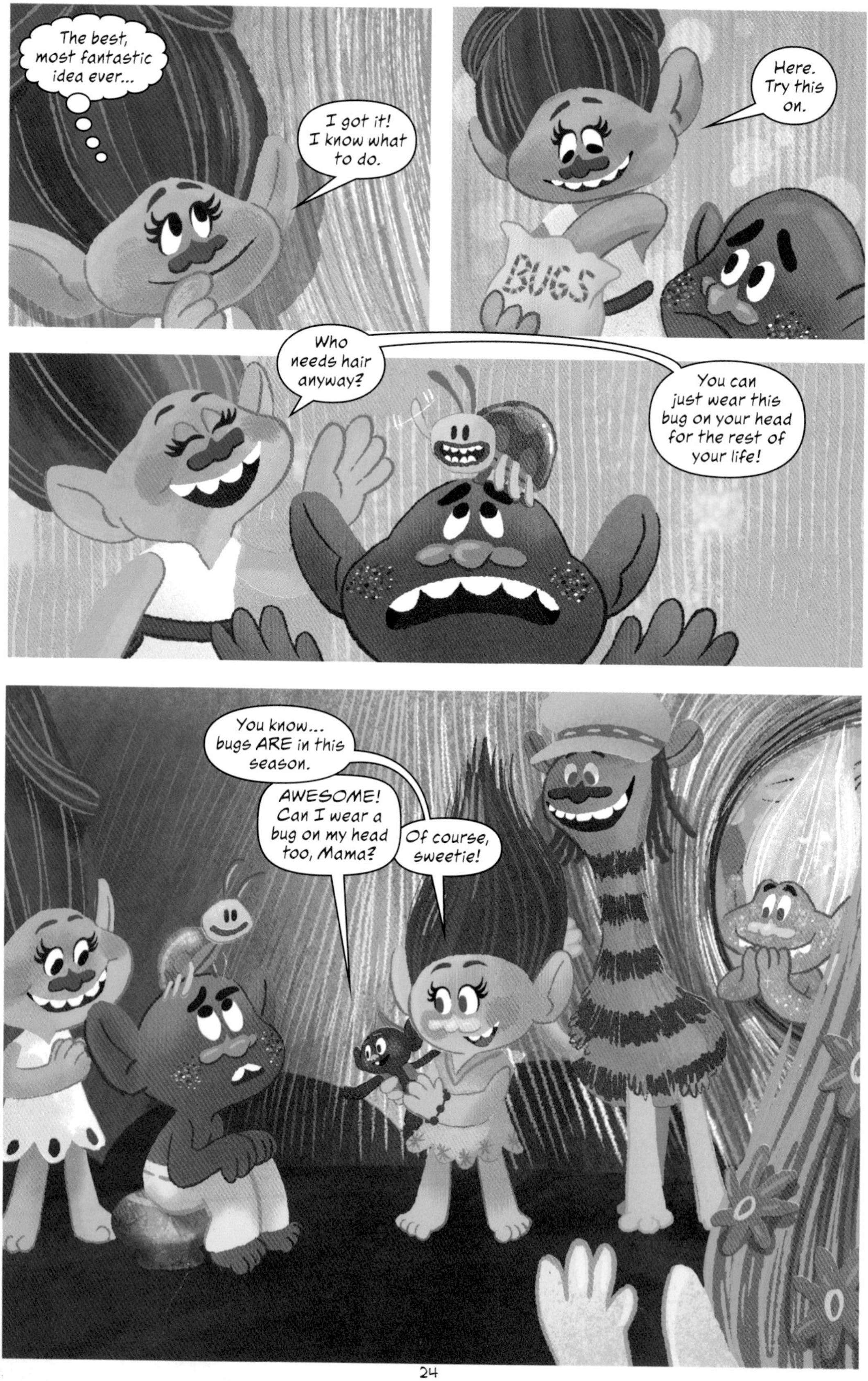
The best, most fantastic idea ever...
I got it! I know what to do.
Here. Try this on.
Who needs hair anyway?
You can just wear this bug on your head for the rest of your life!
You know... bugs ARE in this season.
AWESOME! Can I wear a bug on my head too, Mama?
Of course, sweetie!

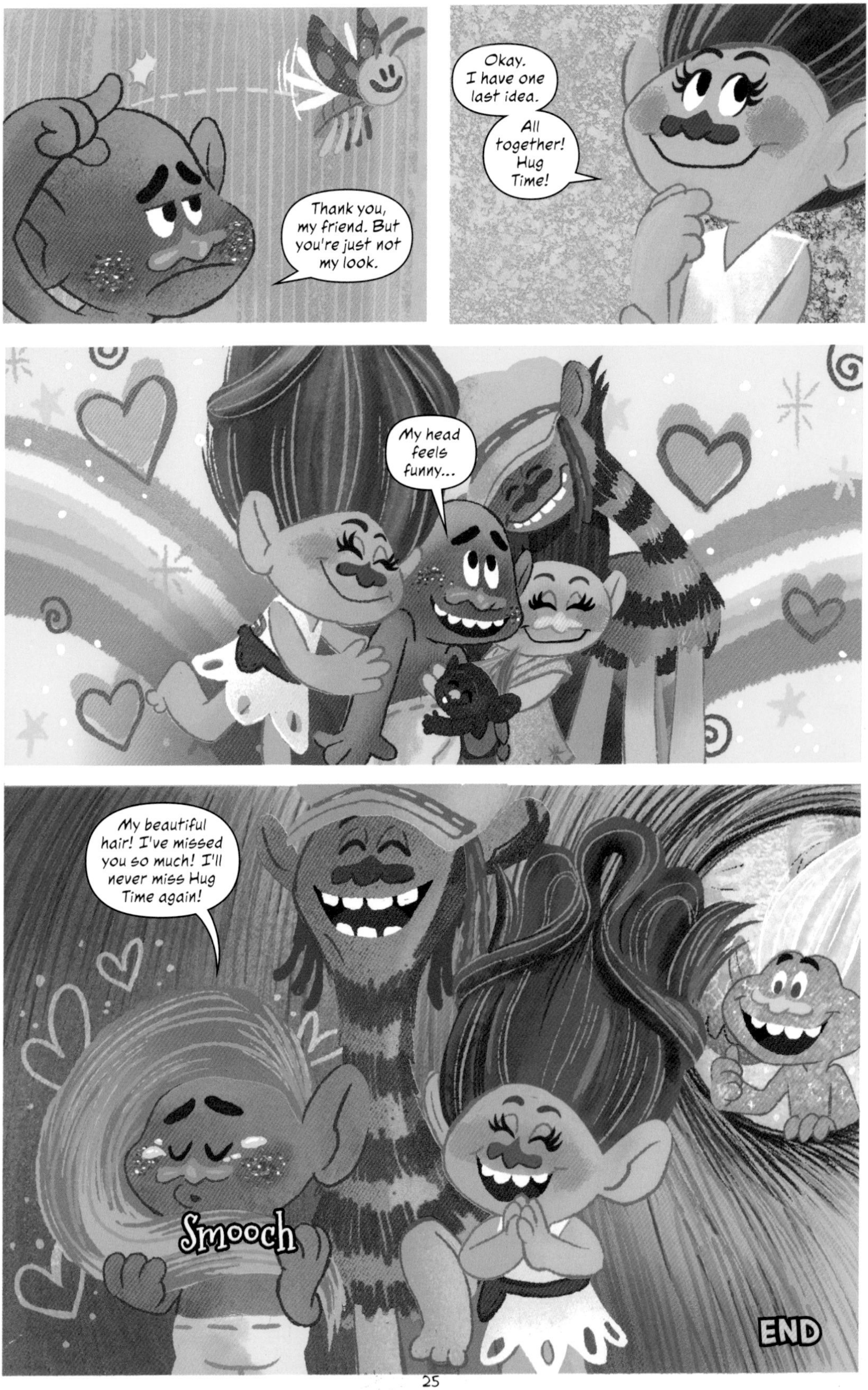

Thank you, my friend. But you're just not my look.
Okay. I have one last idea.
All together! Hug Time!
My head feels funny...
My beautiful hair! I've missed you so much! I'll never miss Hug Time again!
Smooch
END

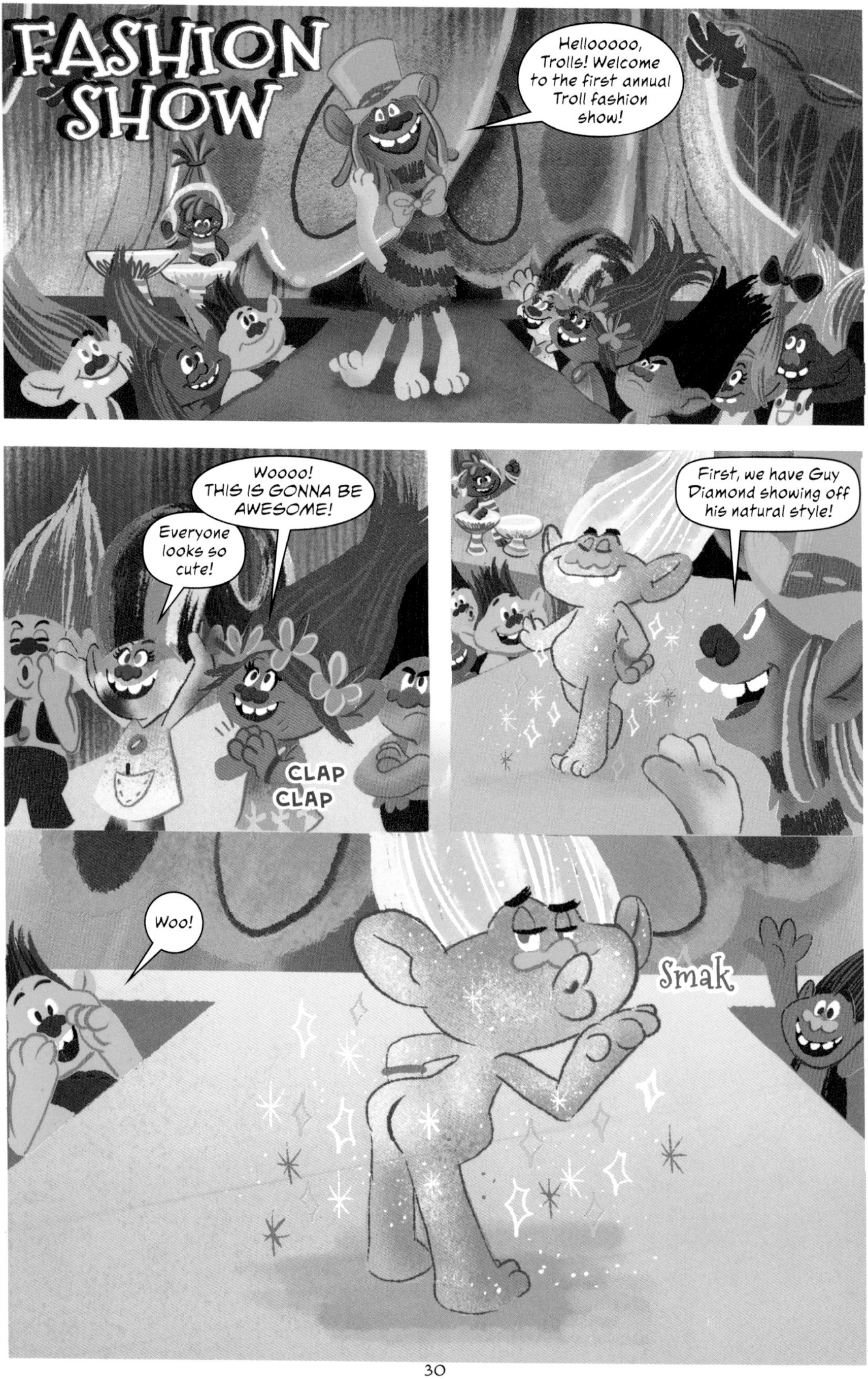
FASHION SHOW
Hellooooo, Trolls! Welcome to the first annual Troll fashion show!
Everyone looks so cute!
Woooo! THIS IS GONNA BE AWESOME!
CLAP CLAP
First, we have Guy Diamond showing off his natural style!
Woo!
Smak

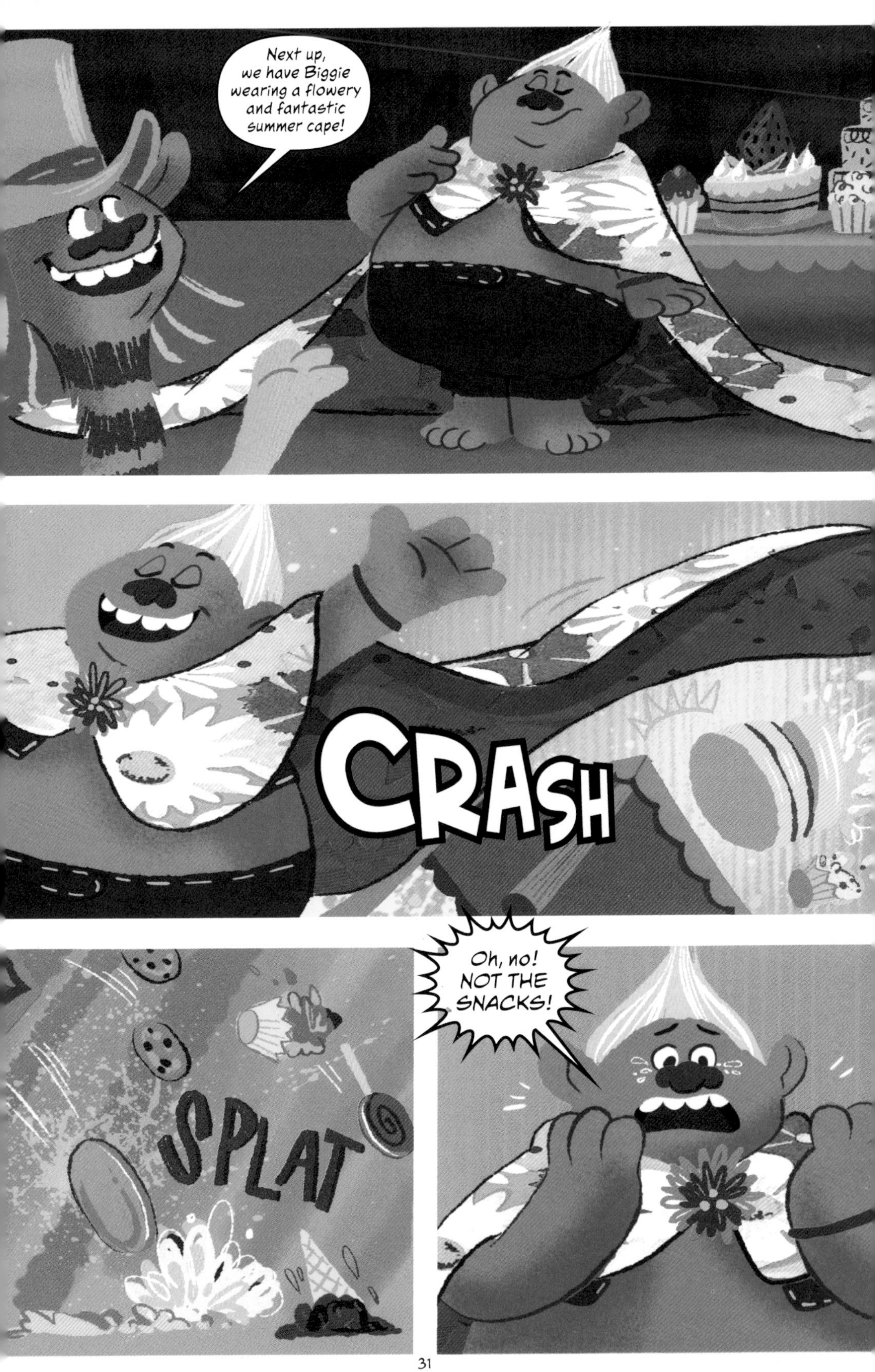
Next up, we have Biggie wearing a flowery and fantastic summer cape!
CRASH
SPLAT
Oh, no! NOT THE SNACKS!

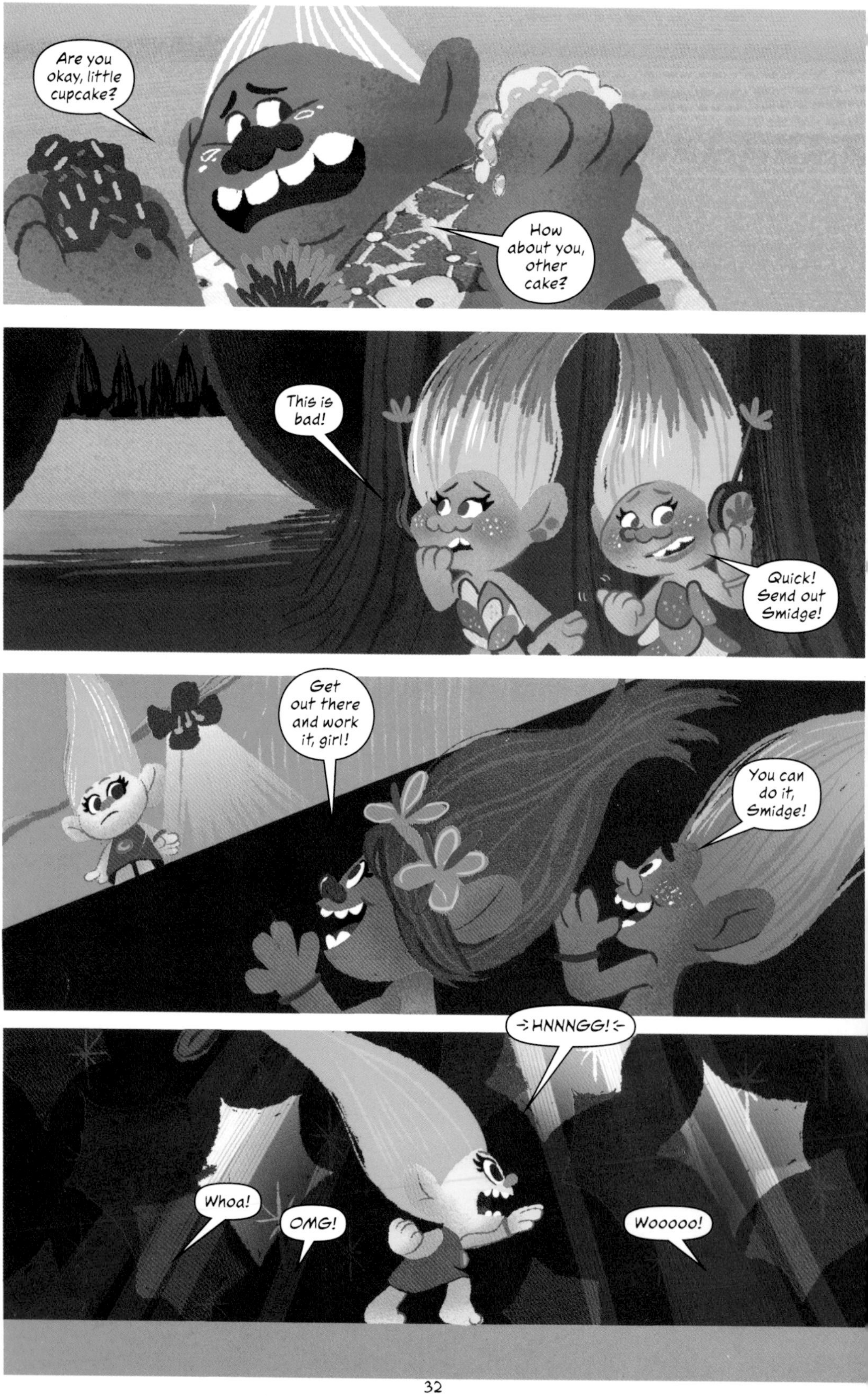
Are you okay, little cupcake?
How about you, other cake?
This is bad!
Quick! Send out Smidge!
Get out there and work it, girl!
You can do it, Smidge!
HNNNGG!
Whoa!
OMG!
Wooooo!

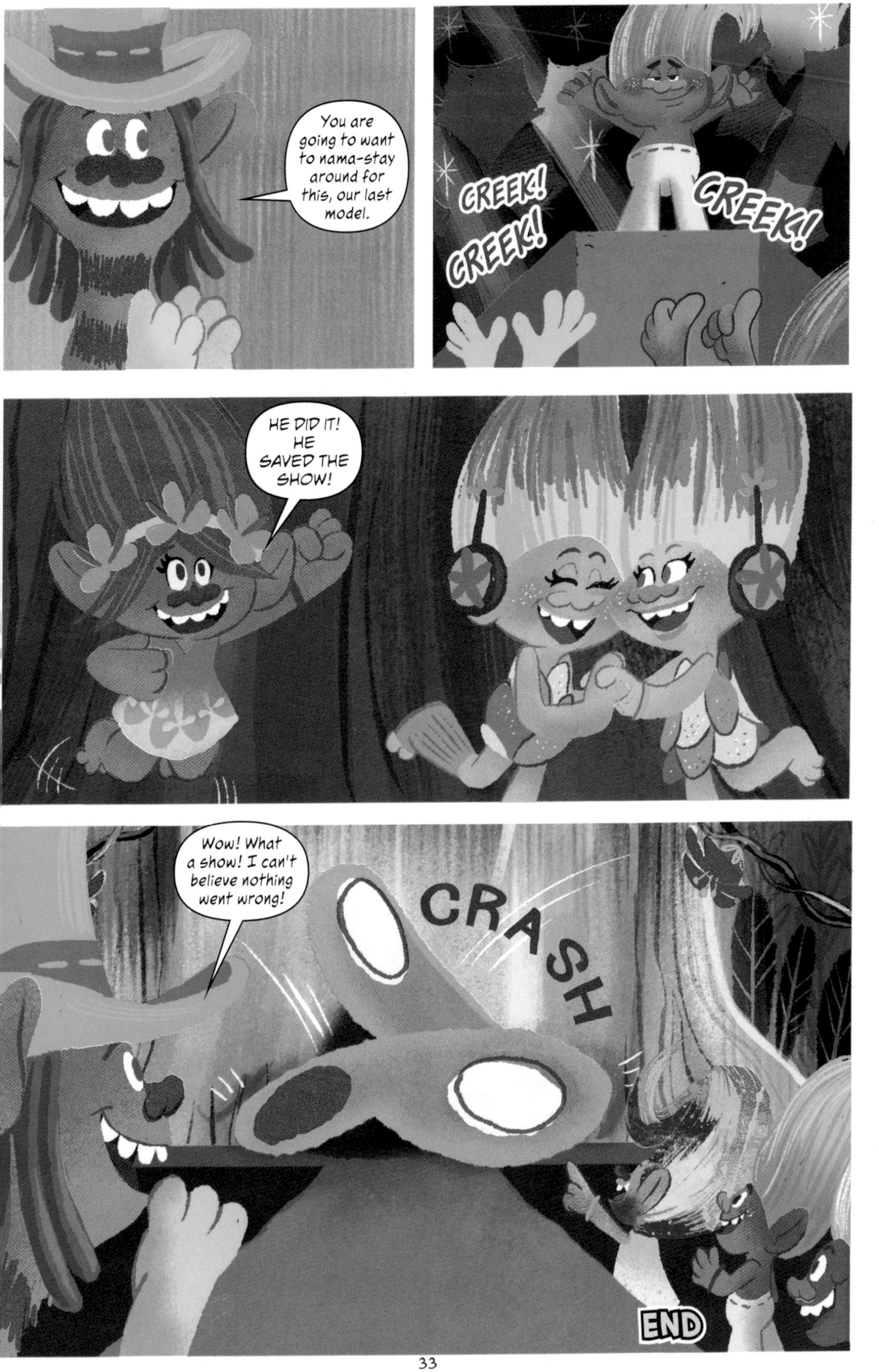
You are going to want to nama-stay around for this, our last model.
CREEK!
CREEK!
CREEK!
HE DID IT! HE SAVED THE SHOW!
Wow! What a show! I can't believe nothing went wrong!
CRASH
END

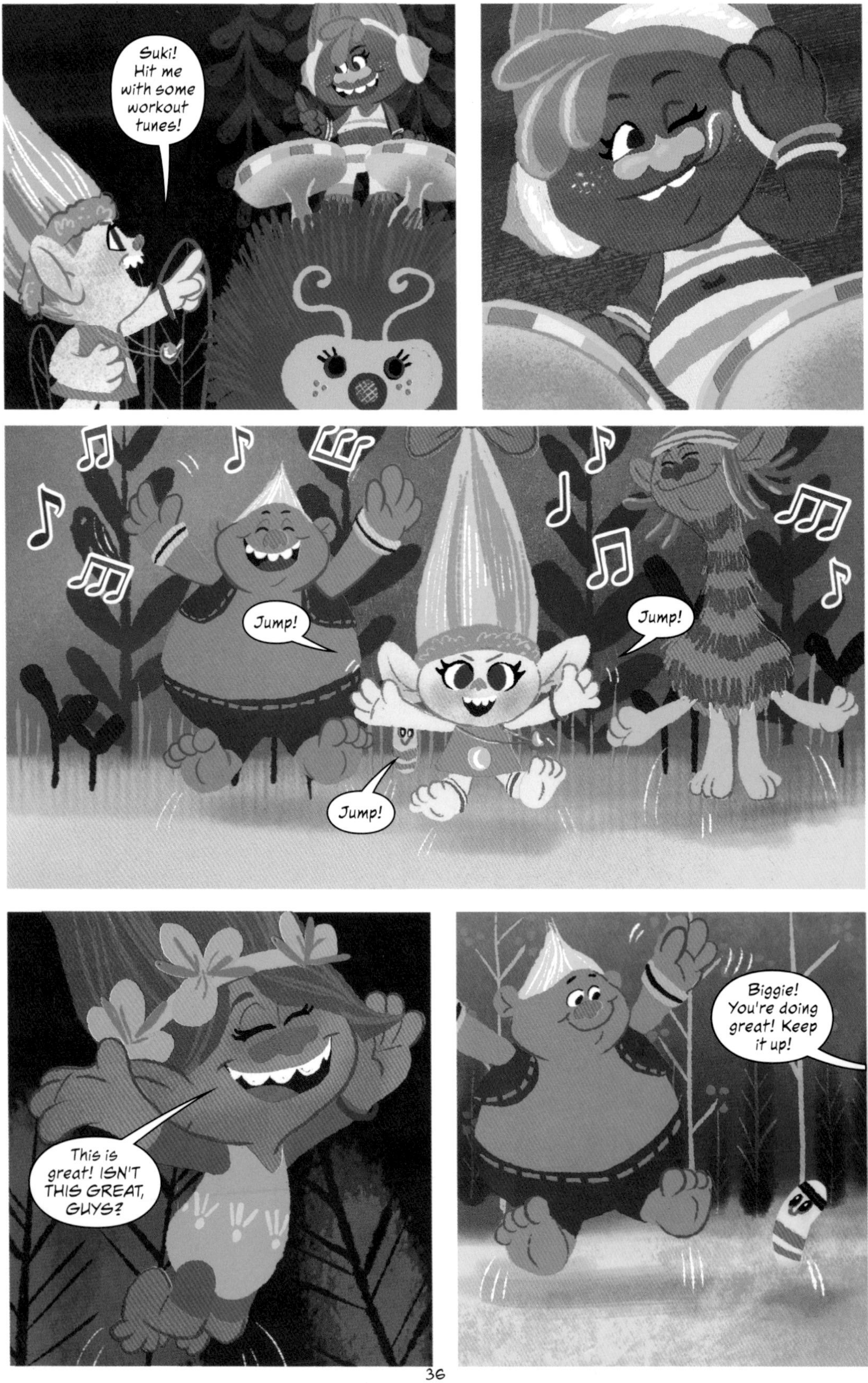

Suki! Hit me with some workout tunes!
Jump!
Jump!
Jump!
This is great! ISN'T THIS GREAT, GUYS?
Biggie! You're doing great! Keep it up!

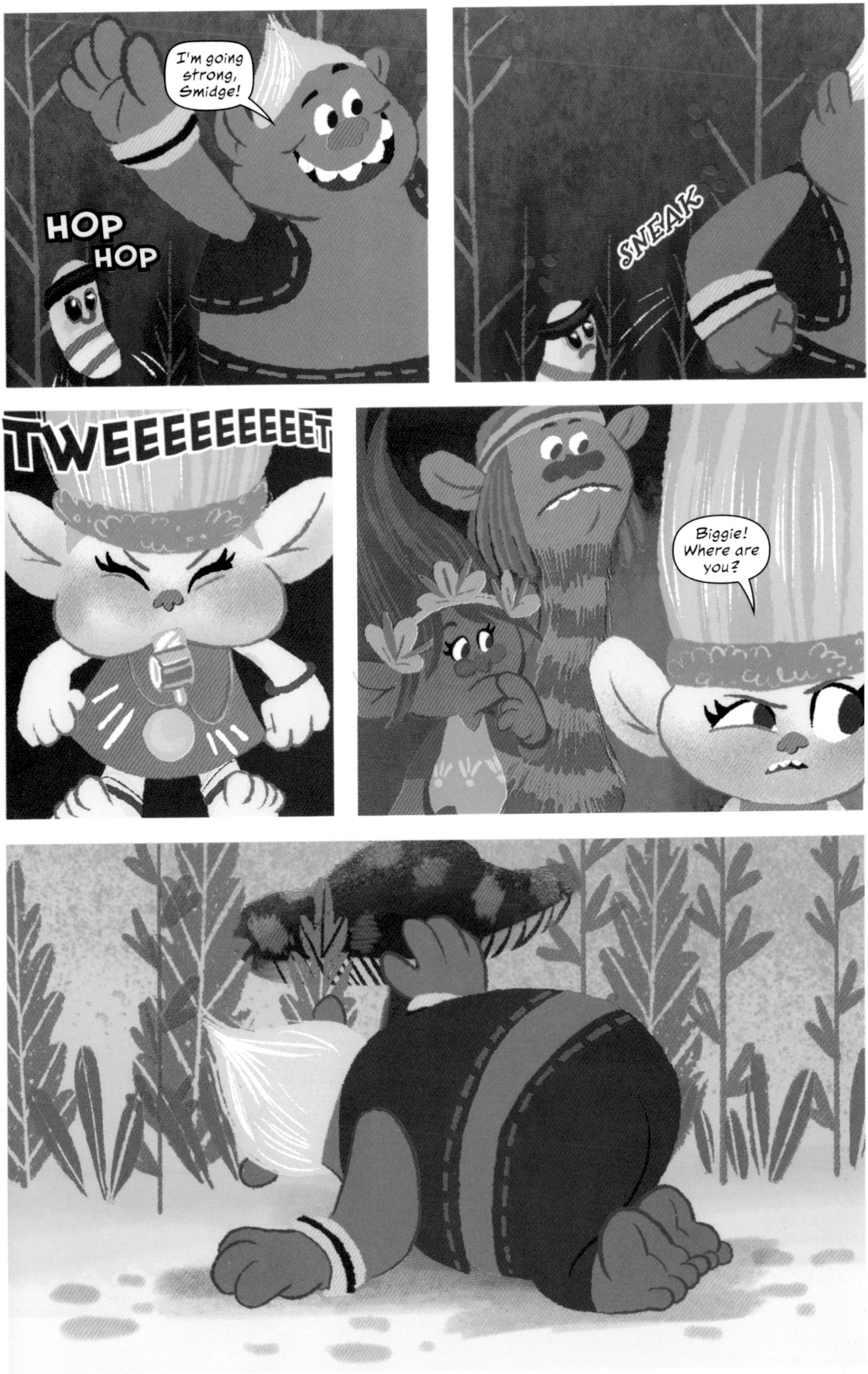
I'm going strong, Smidge!
HOP
HOP
SNEAK
TWEEEEEEEEET
Biggie! Where are you?

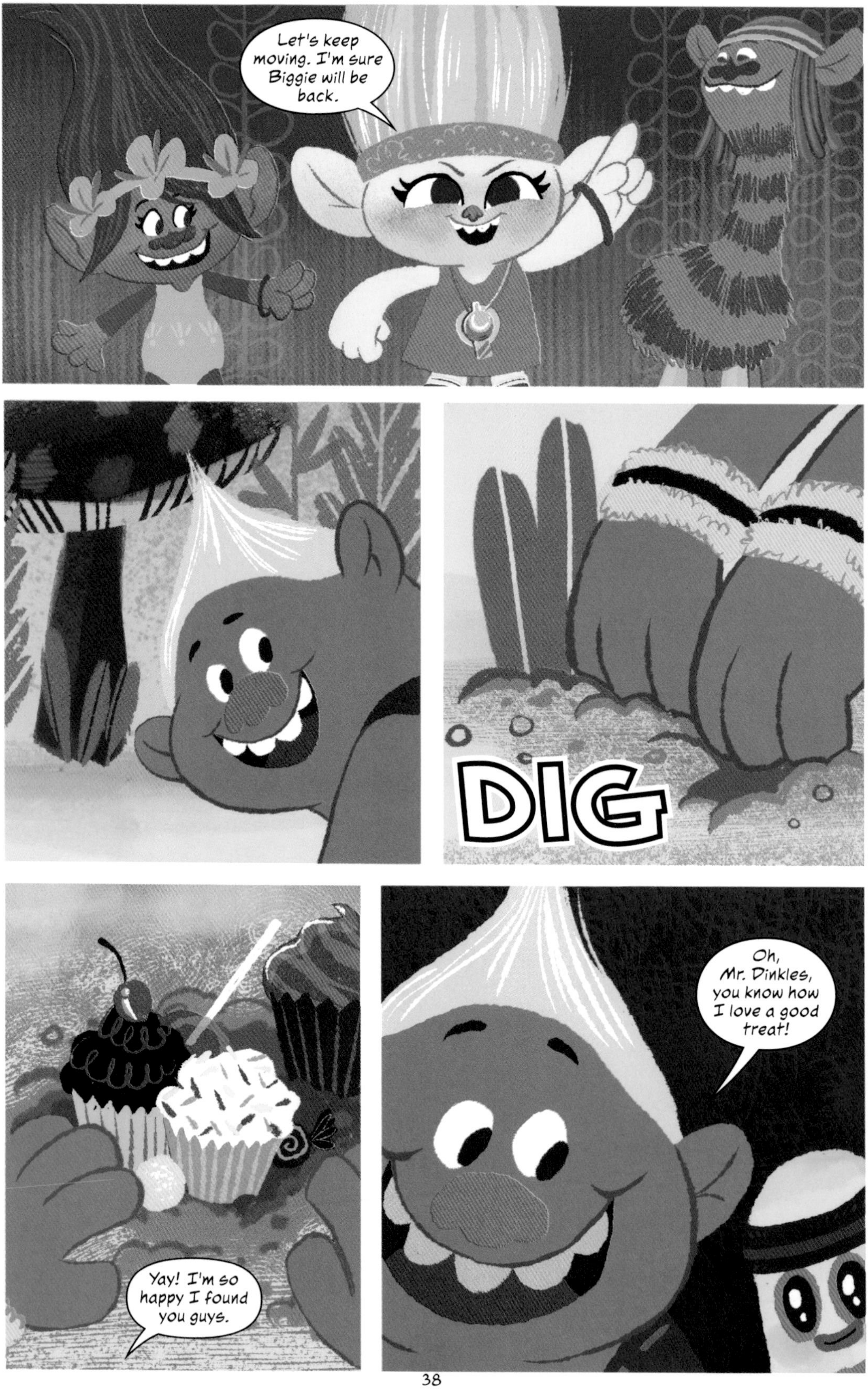
Let's keep moving. I'm sure Biggie will be back.
DIG
Yay! I'm so happy I found you guys.
Oh, Mr. Dinkles, you know how I love a good treat!

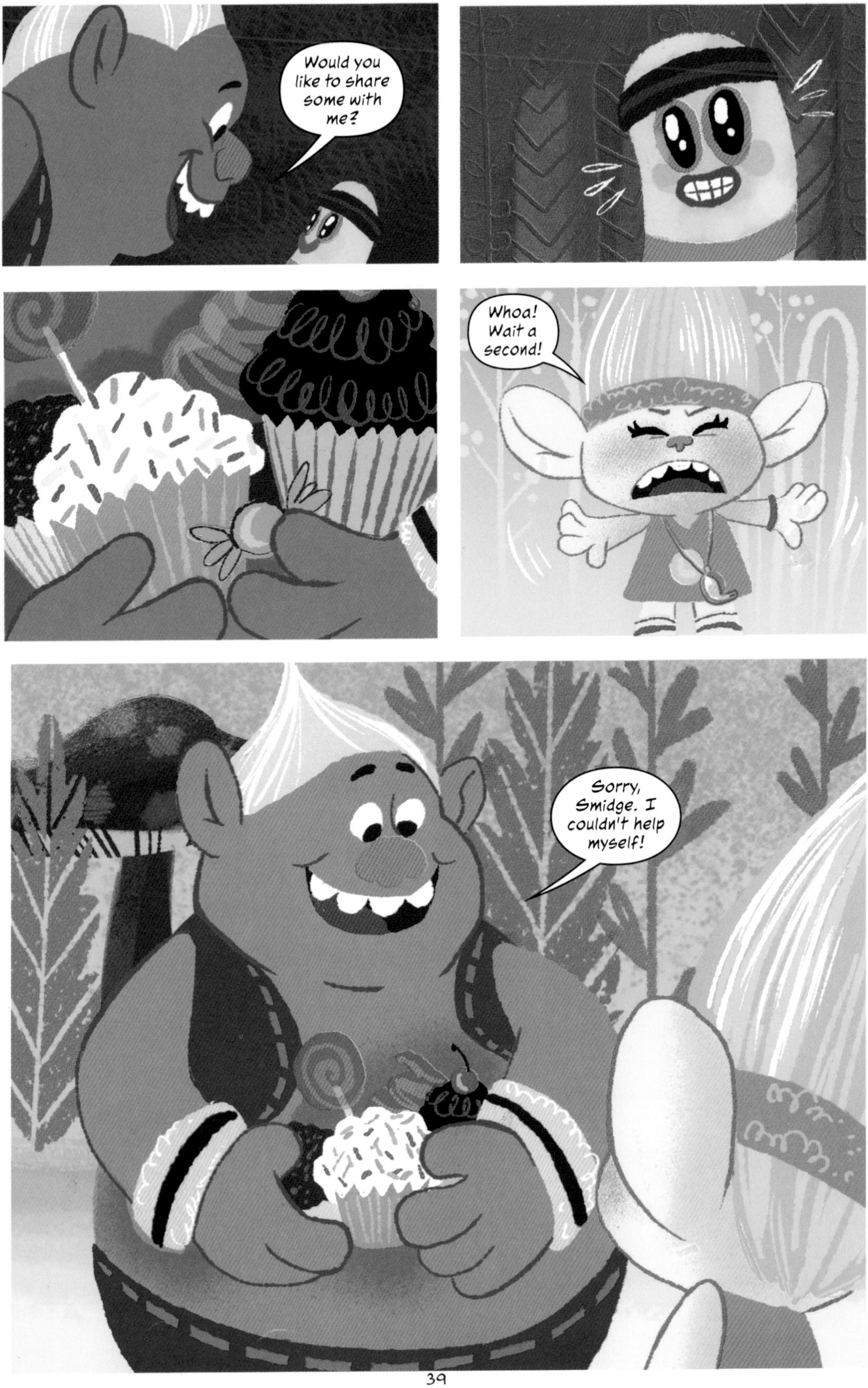

Would you like to share some with me?
Whoa! Wait a second!
Sorry, Smidge. I couldn't help myself!

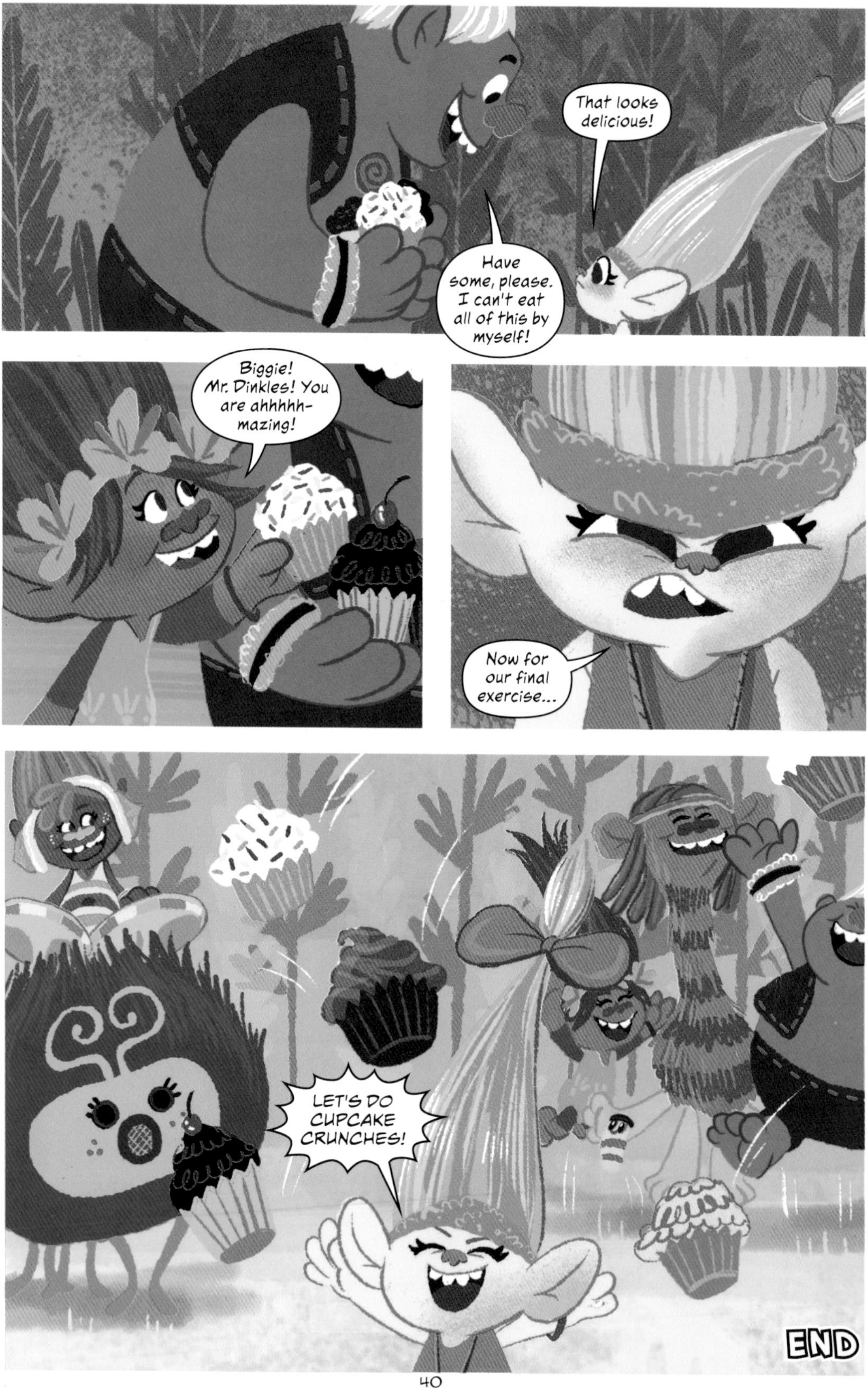
That looks delicious!
Have some, please. I can't eat all of this by myself!
Biggie! Mr. Dinkles! You are ahhhhh-mazing!
Now for our final exercise...
LET'S DO CUPCAKE CRUNCHES!
END

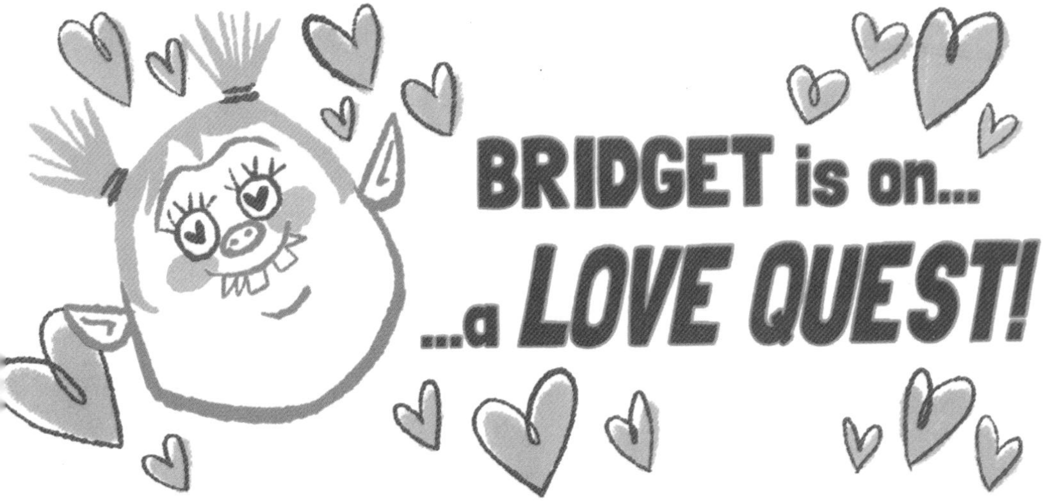
BRIDGET is on...
...a LOVE QUEST!

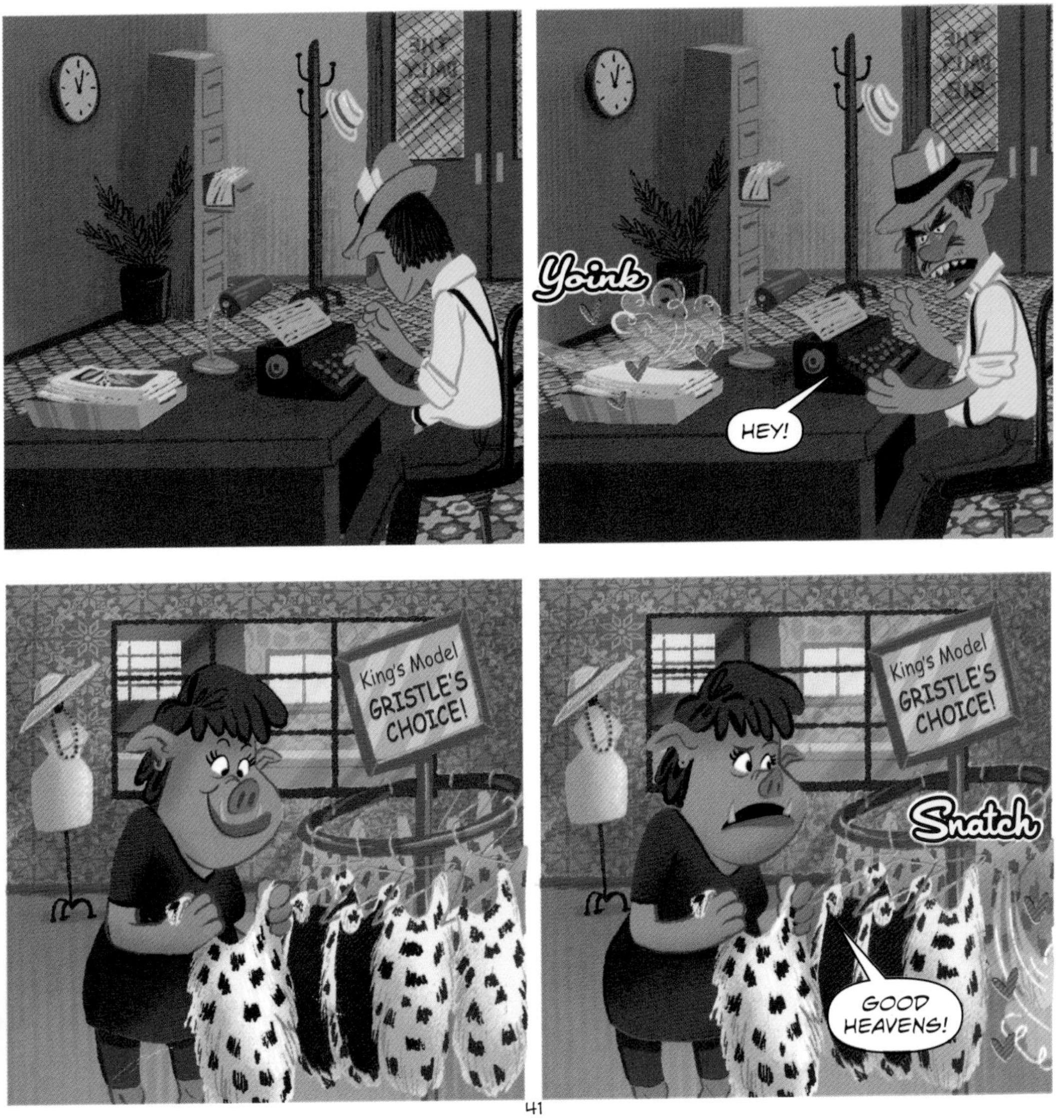
Yoink
HEY!
King's Model
GRISTLE'S CHOICE!
King's Model
GRISTLE'S CHOICE!
Snatch
GOOD HEAVENS!

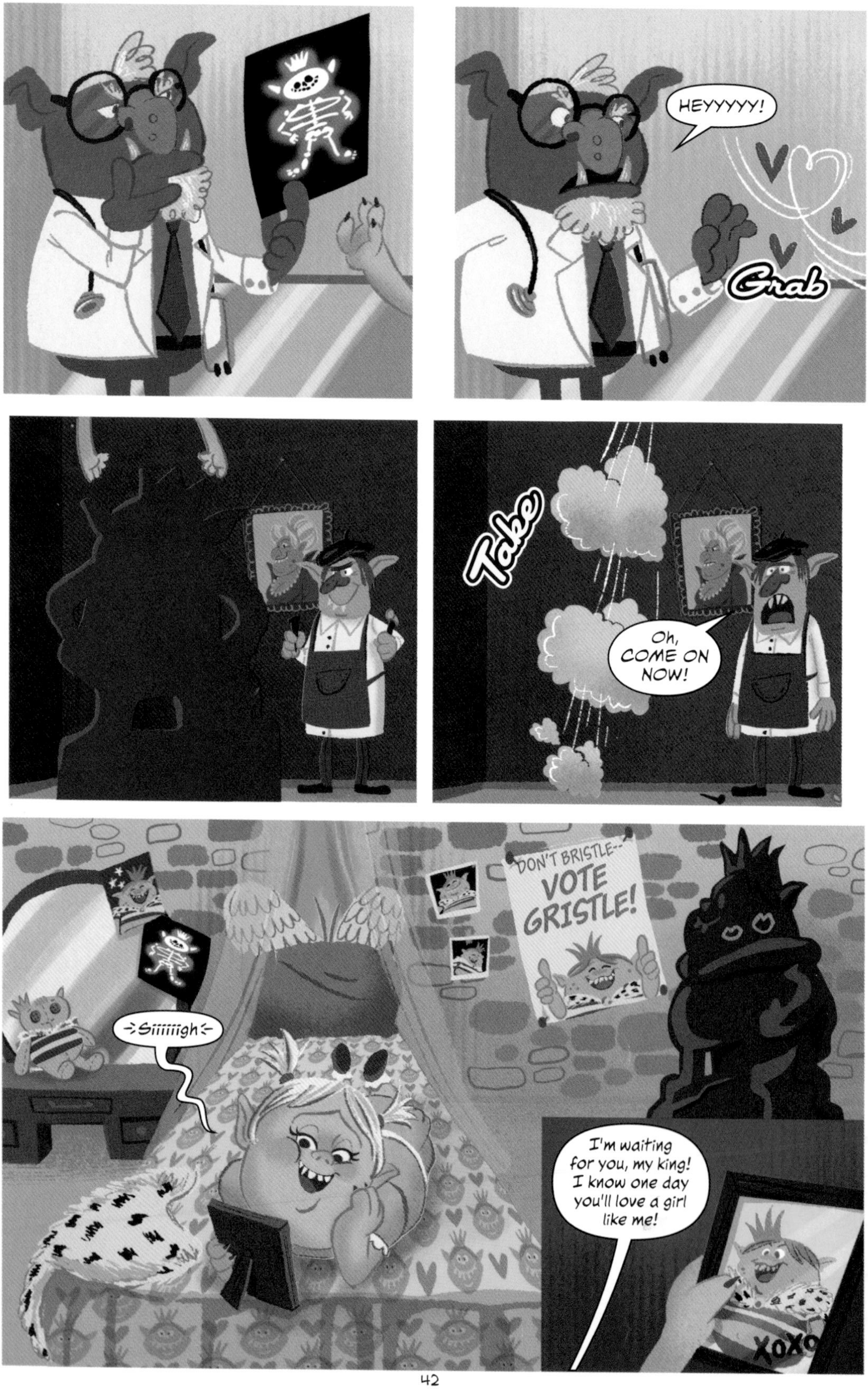
HEYYYYY!
Grab
Take
Oh, COME ON NOW!
DON'T BRISTLE--
VOTE GRISTLE!
Siiiiiigh
I'm waiting for you, my king! I know one day you'll love a girl like me!
XOXO

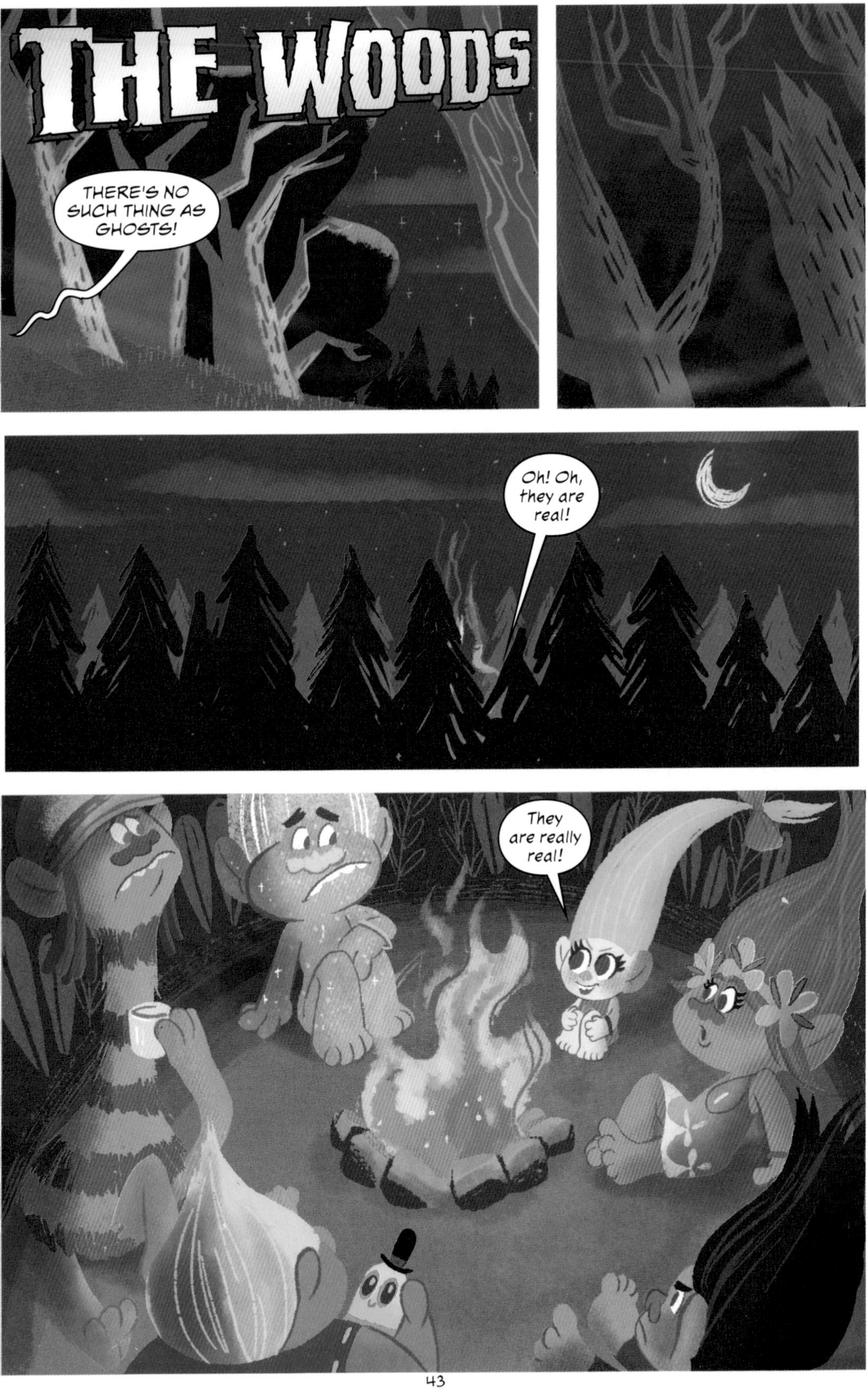
THE WOODS
THERE'S NO SUCH THING AS GHOSTS!
Oh! Oh, they are real!
They are really real!

46

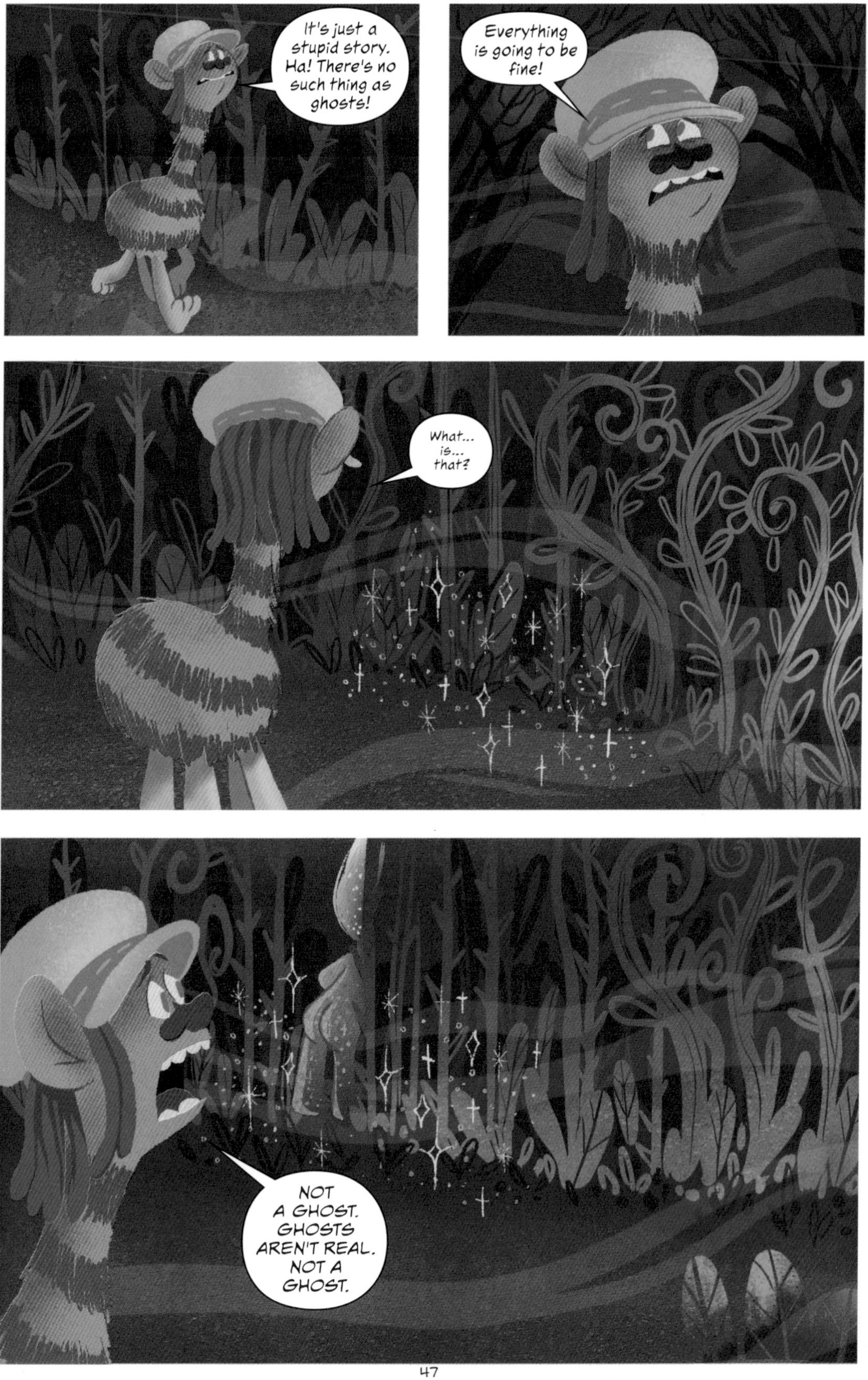
It's just a stupid story. Ha! There's no such thing as ghosts!
Everything is going to be fine!
What... is... that?
NOT A GHOST. GHOSTS AREN'T REAL. NOT A GHOST.

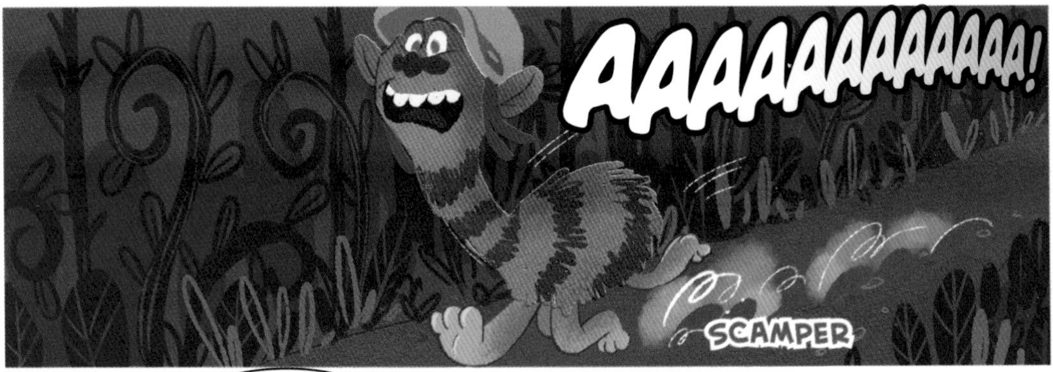
AAAAAAAAAAAA!
SCAMPER

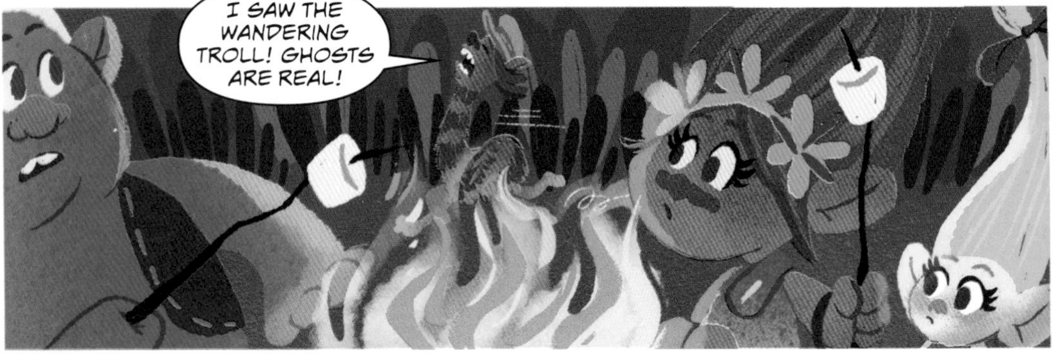
I SAW THE WANDERING TROLL! GHOSTS ARE REAL!

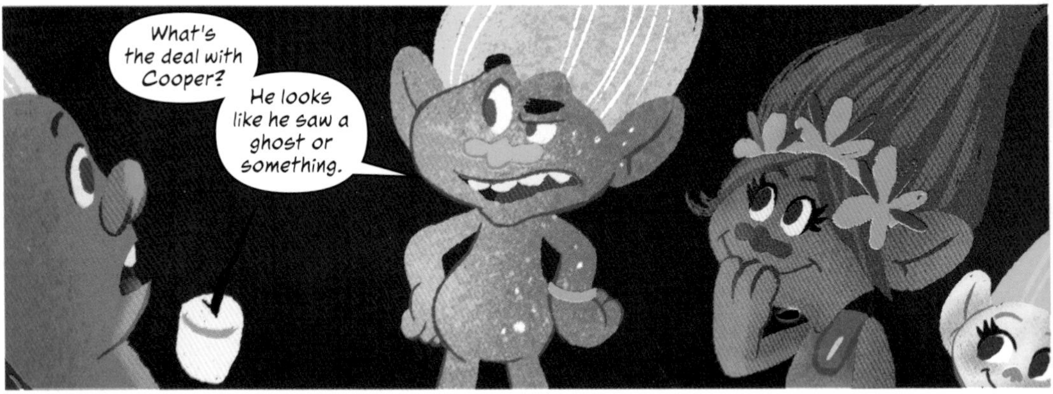
What's the deal with Cooper?
He looks like he saw a ghost or something.

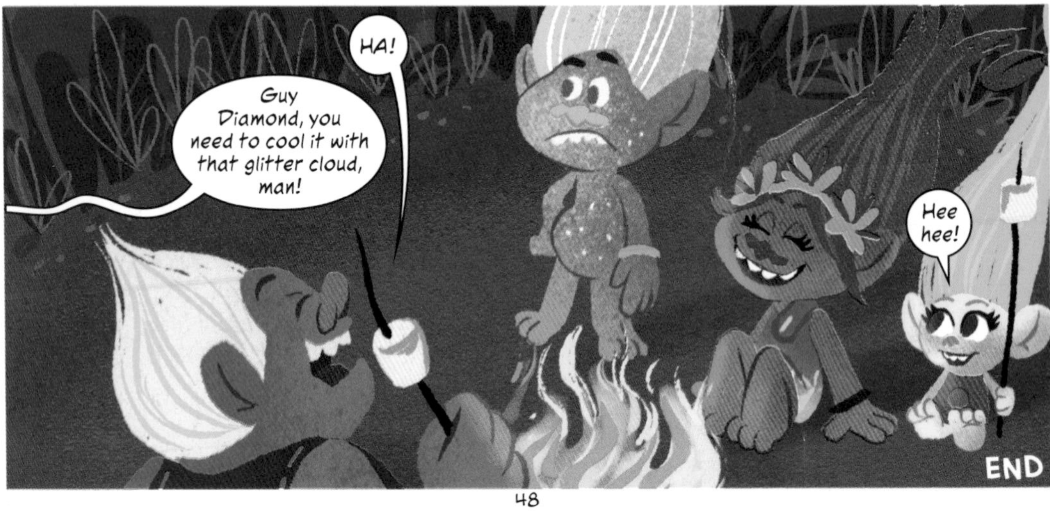
HA!
Guy Diamond, you need to cool it with that glitter cloud, man!
Hee hee!
END

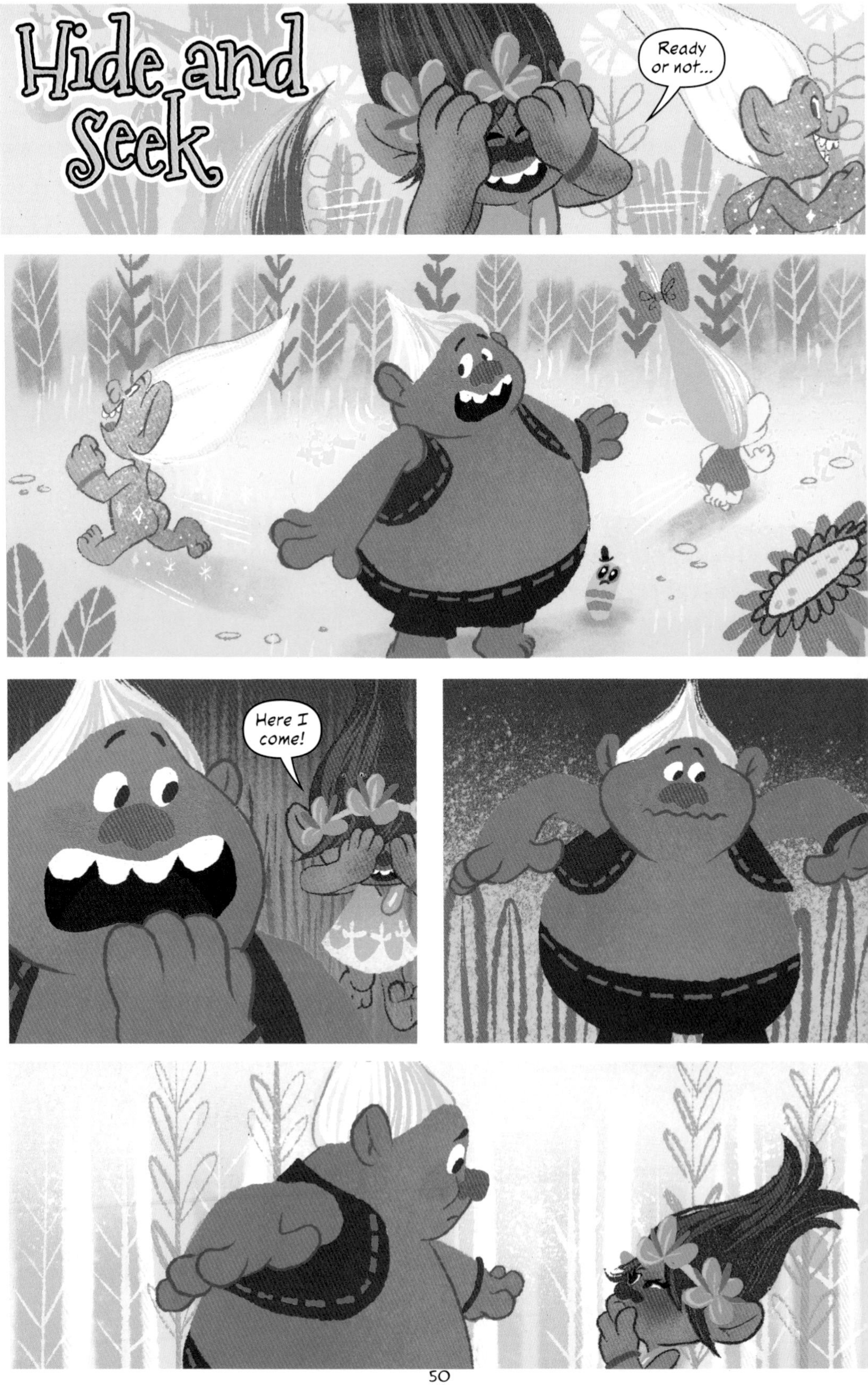
Hide and Seek
Ready or not...
Here I come!

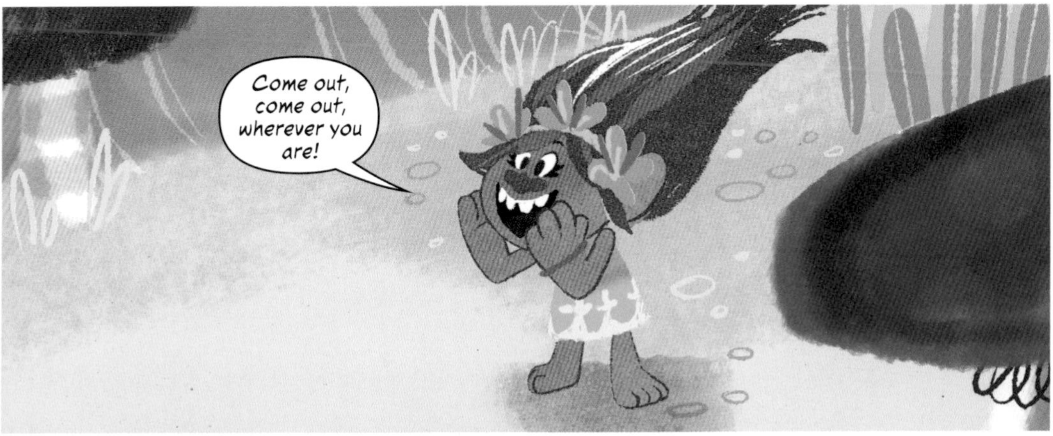
Come out, come out, wherever you are!
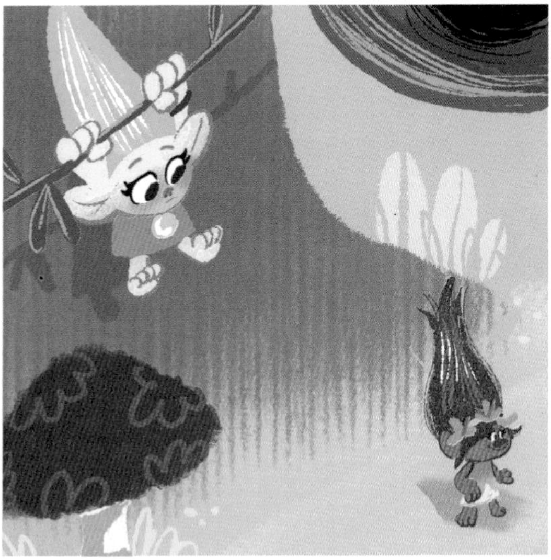
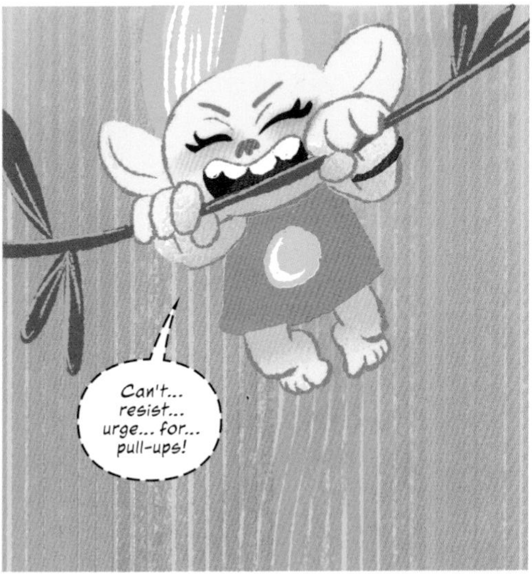
Can't... resist... urge... for... pull-ups!
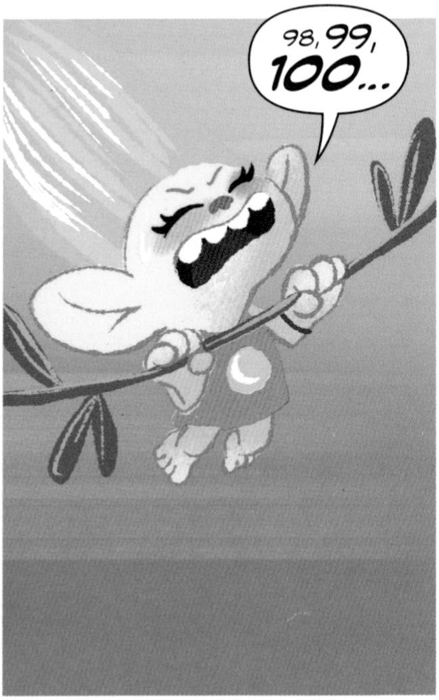
98, 99, 100...
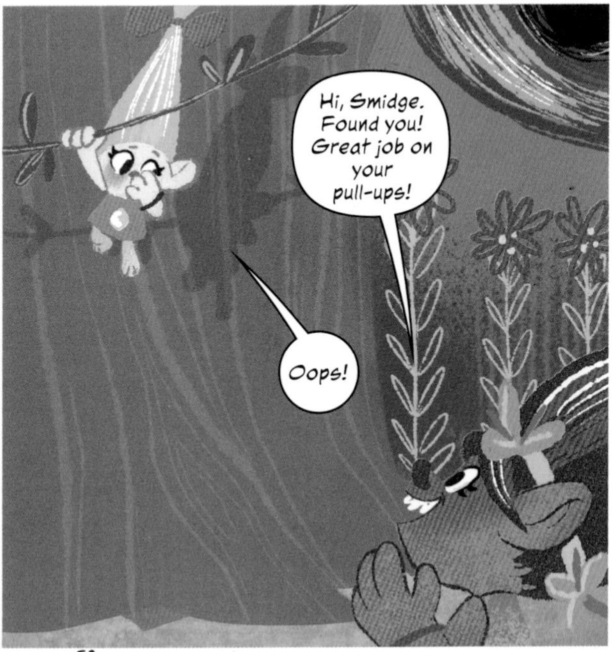
Hi, Smidge. Found you! Great job on your pull-ups!
Oops!

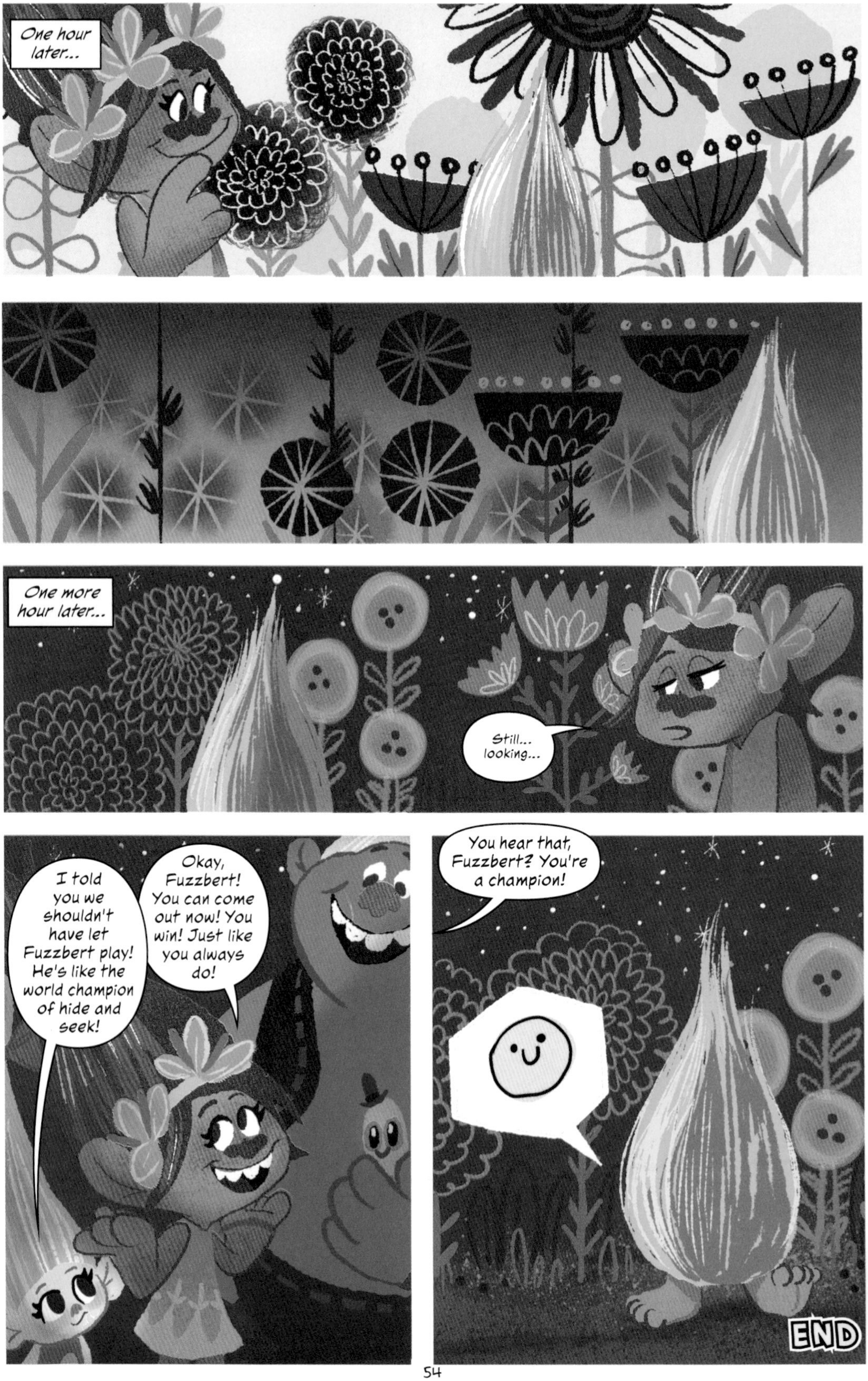
One hour later...
One more hour later...
Still... looking...
I told you we shouldn't have let Fuzzbert play! He's like the world champion of hide and seek!
Okay, Fuzzbert! You can come out now! You win! Just like you always do!
You hear that, Fuzzbert? You're a champion!
END

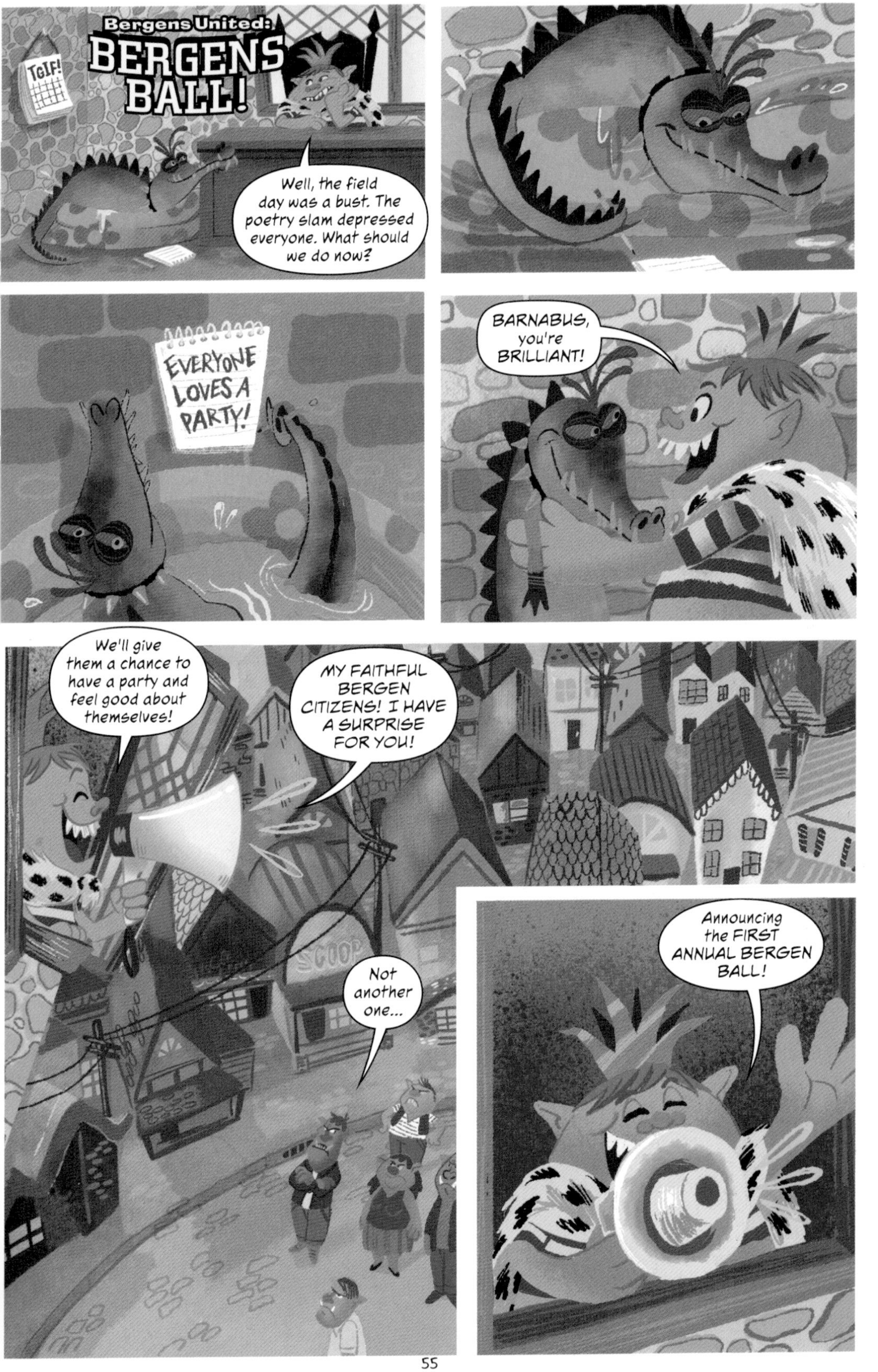
Bergens United:
BERGENS BALL!
TGIF!
Well, the field day was a bust. The poetry slam depressed everyone. What should we do now?
EVERYONE LOVES A PARTY!
BARNABUS, you're BRILLIANT!
We'll give them a chance to have a party and feel good about themselves!
MY FAITHFUL BERGEN CITIZENS! I HAVE A SURPRISE FOR YOU!
SCOOP
Not another one...
Announcing the FIRST ANNUAL BERGEN BALL!

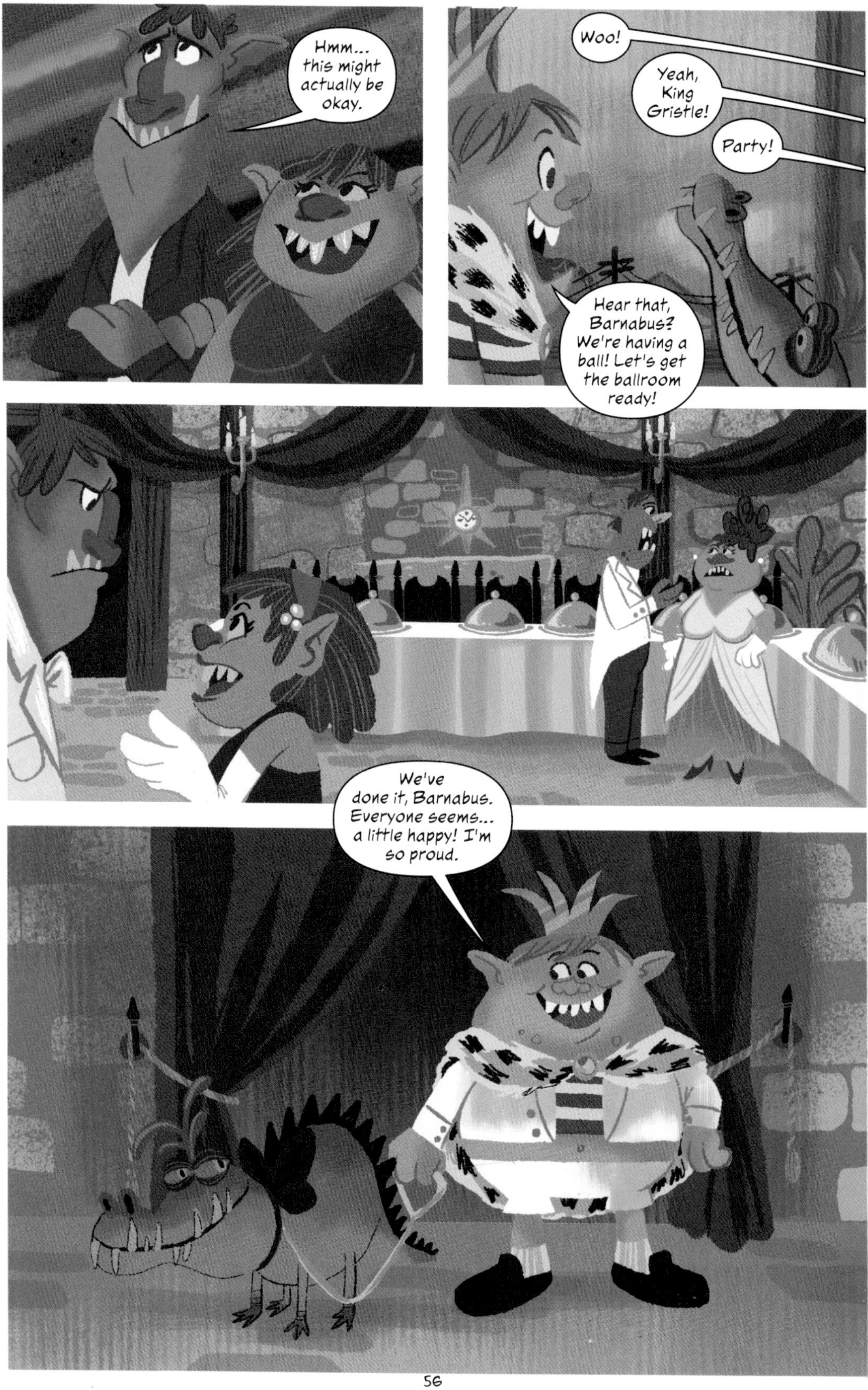

Hmm... this might actually be okay.
Woo!
Yeah, King Gristle!
Party!
Hear that, Barnabus? We're having a ball! Let's get the ballroom ready!
We've done it, Barnabus. Everyone seems... a little happy! I'm so proud.

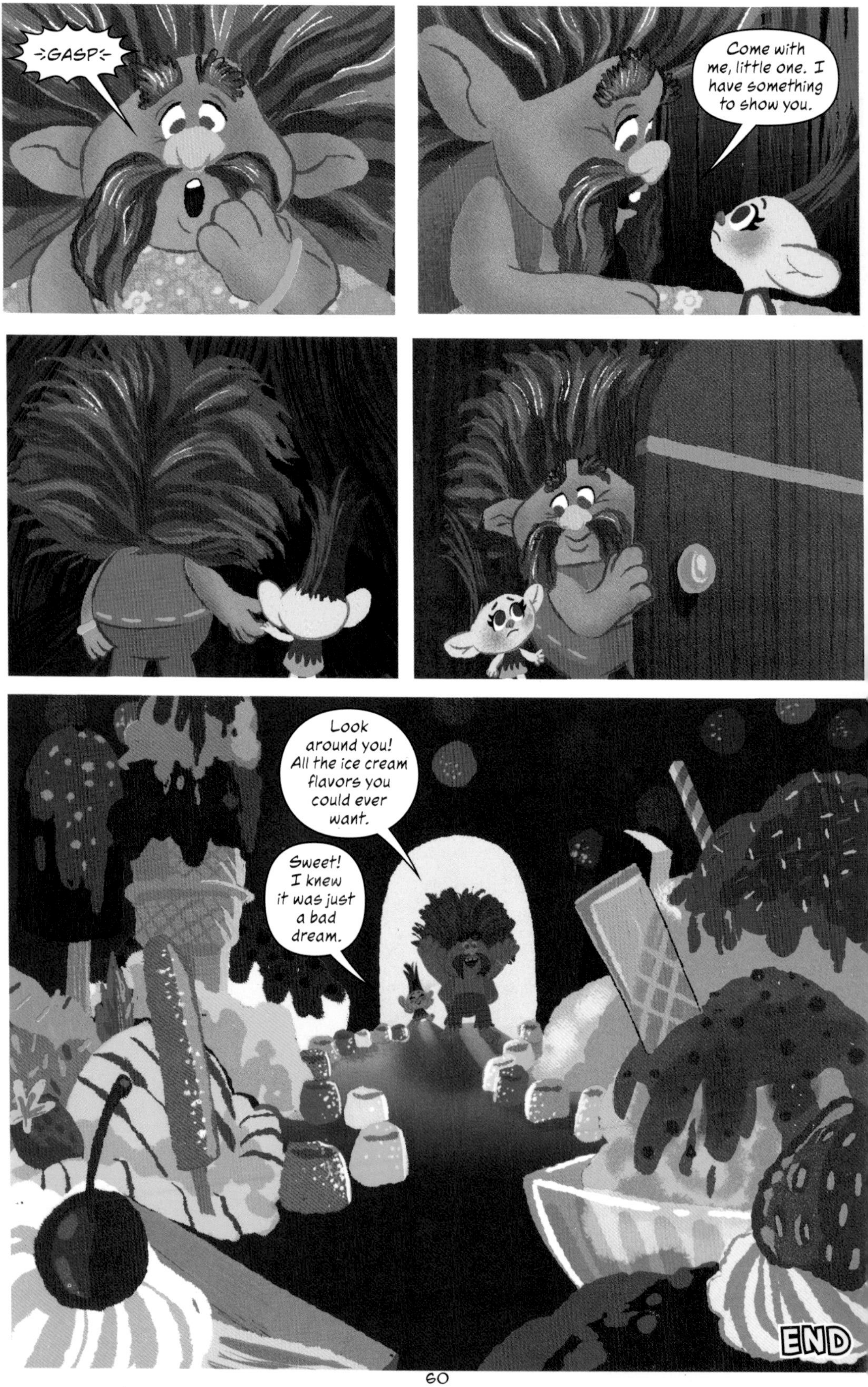
-GASP-
Come with me, little one. I have something to show you.
Look around you! All the ice cream flavors you could ever want.
Sweet! I knew it was just a bad dream.
END

Special Preview of DANCE CLASS #8 "Snow White and the Seven Dwarves"!

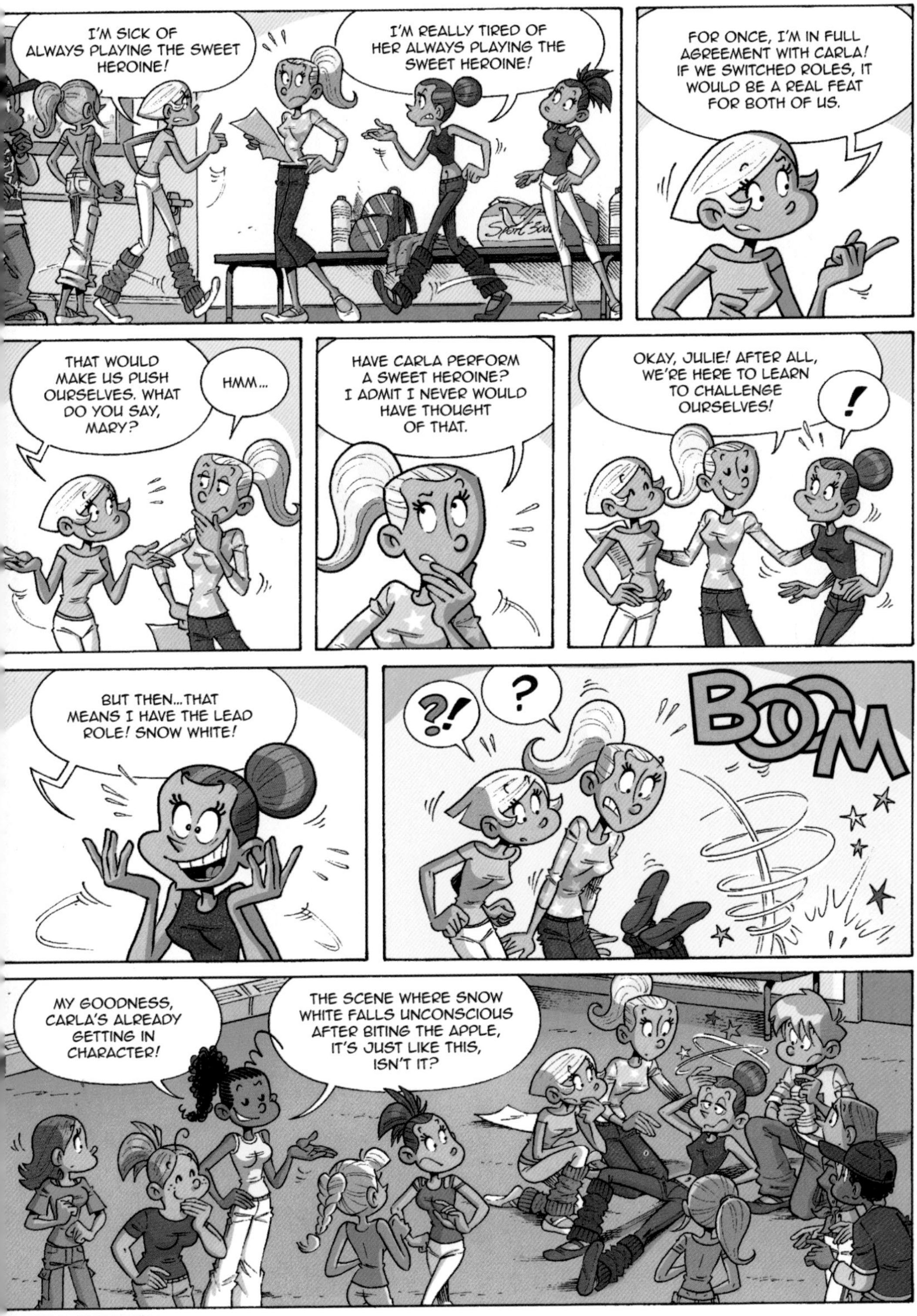

I'M SICK OF ALWAYS PLAYING THE SWEET HEROINE!
I'M REALLY TIRED OF HER ALWAYS PLAYING THE SWEET HEROINE!
FOR ONCE, I'M IN FULL AGREEMENT WITH CARLA! IF WE SWITCHED ROLES, IT WOULD BE A REAL FEAT FOR BOTH OF US.
THAT WOULD MAKE US PUSH OURSELVES. WHAT DO YOU SAY, MARY?
HMM...
HAVE CARLA PERFORM A SWEET HEROINE? I ADMIT I NEVER WOULD HAVE THOUGHT OF THAT.
OKAY, JULIE! AFTER ALL, WE'RE HERE TO LEARN TO CHALLENGE OURSELVES!
!
BUT THEN...THAT MEANS I HAVE THE LEAD ROLE! SNOW WHITE!
?!
?
BOOM
MY GOODNESS, CARLA'S ALREADY GETTING IN CHARACTER!
THE SCENE WHERE SNOW WHITE FALLS UNCONSCIOUS AFTER BITING THE APPLE, IT'S JUST LIKE THIS, ISN'T IT?

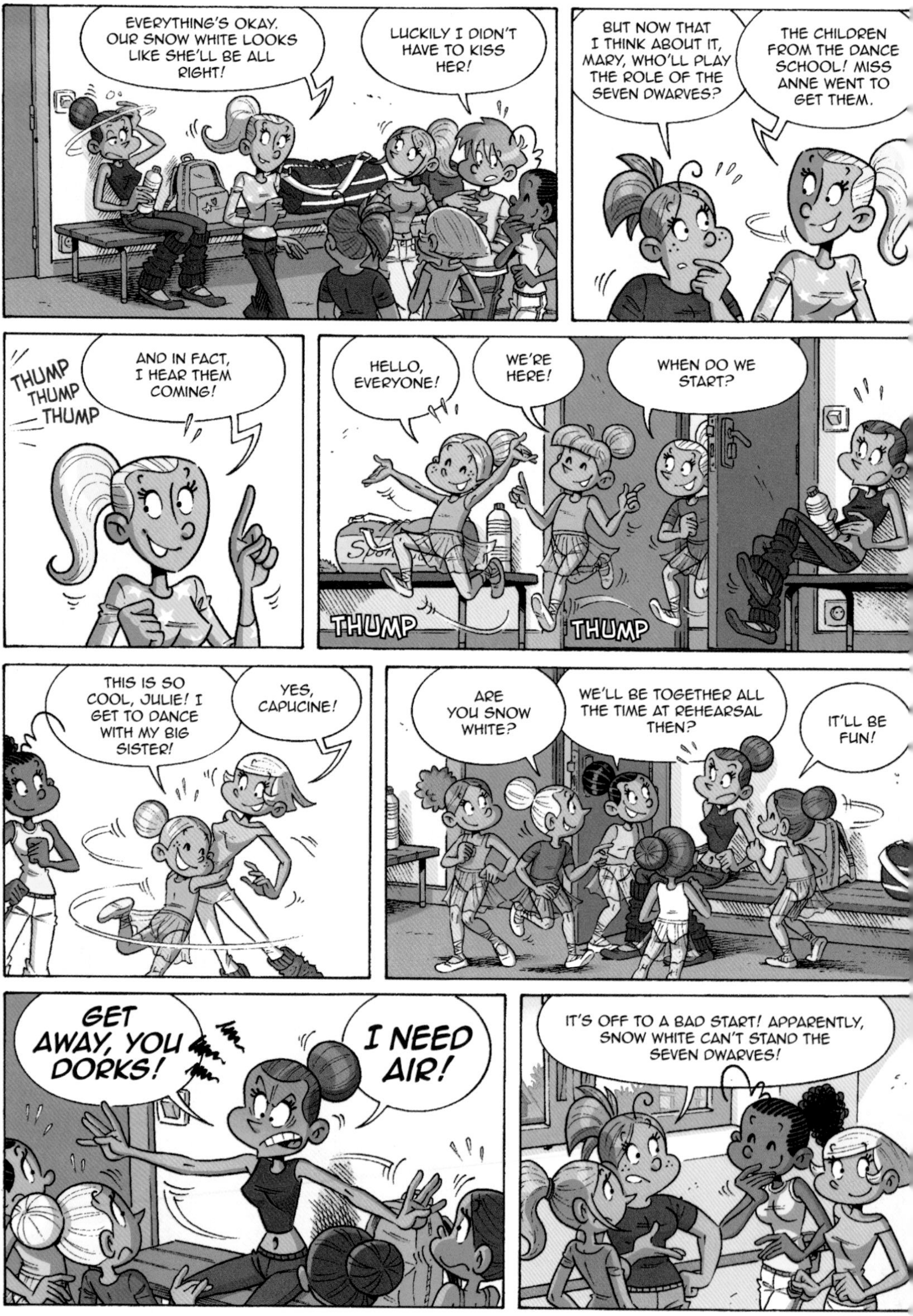
EVERYTHING'S OKAY. OUR SNOW WHITE LOOKS LIKE SHE'LL BE ALL RIGHT!
LUCKILY I DIDN'T HAVE TO KISS HER!
BUT NOW THAT I THINK ABOUT IT, MARY, WHO'LL PLAY THE ROLE OF THE SEVEN DWARVES?
THE CHILDREN FROM THE DANCE SCHOOL! MISS ANNE WENT TO GET THEM.
THUMP THUMP THUMP
AND IN FACT, I HEAR THEM COMING!
HELLO, EVERYONE!
WE'RE HERE!
WHEN DO WE START?
THUMP
THUMP
THIS IS SO COOL, JULIE! I GET TO DANCE WITH MY BIG SISTER!
YES, CAPUCINE!
ARE YOU SNOW WHITE?
WE'LL BE TOGETHER ALL THE TIME AT REHEARSAL THEN?
IT'LL BE FUN!
GET AWAY, YOU DORKS!
I NEED AIR!
IT'S OFF TO A BAD START! APPARENTLY, SNOW WHITE CAN'T STAND THE SEVEN DWARVES!

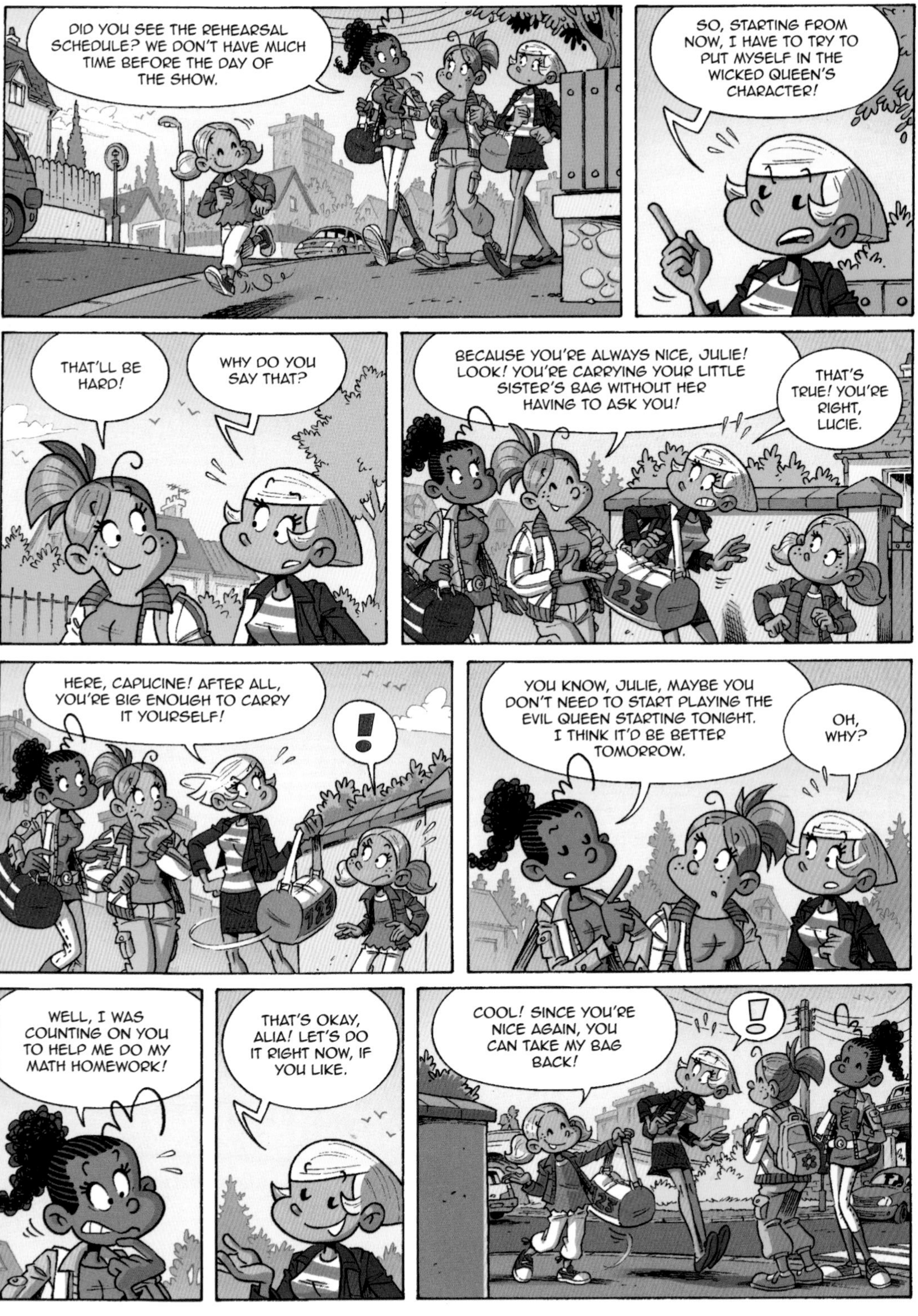
DID YOU SEE THE REHEARSAL SCHEDULE? WE DON'T HAVE MUCH TIME BEFORE THE DAY OF THE SHOW.
SO, STARTING FROM NOW, I HAVE TO TRY TO PUT MYSELF IN THE WICKED QUEEN'S CHARACTER!
THAT'LL BE HARD!
WHY DO YOU SAY THAT?
BECAUSE YOU'RE ALWAYS NICE, JULIE! LOOK! YOU'RE CARRYING YOUR LITTLE SISTER'S BAG WITHOUT HER HAVING TO ASK YOU!
THAT'S TRUE! YOU'RE RIGHT, LUCIE.
HERE, CAPUCINE! AFTER ALL, YOU'RE BIG ENOUGH TO CARRY IT YOURSELF!
!
YOU KNOW, JULIE, MAYBE YOU DON'T NEED TO START PLAYING THE EVIL QUEEN STARTING TONIGHT. I THINK IT'D BE BETTER TOMORROW.
OH, WHY?
WELL, I WAS COUNTING ON YOU TO HELP ME DO MY MATH HOMEWORK!
THAT'S OKAY, ALIA! LET'S DO IT RIGHT NOW, IF YOU LIKE.
COOL! SINCE YOU'RE NICE AGAIN, YOU CAN TAKE MY BAG BACK!
!

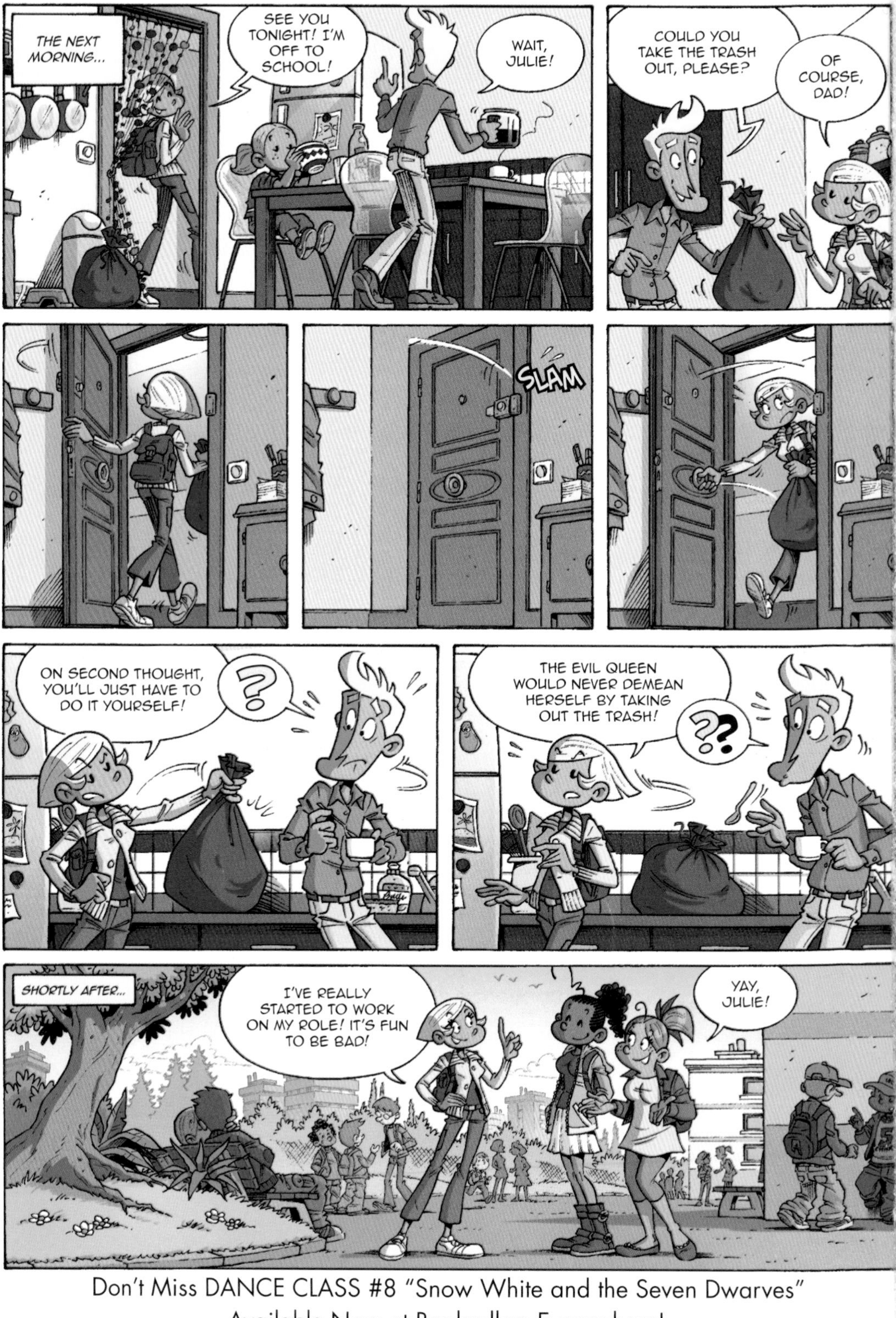
THE NEXT MORNING...
SEE YOU TONIGHT! I'M OFF TO SCHOOL!
WAIT, JULIE!
COULD YOU TAKE THE TRASH OUT, PLEASE?
OF COURSE, DAD!
SLAM
ON SECOND THOUGHT, YOU'LL JUST HAVE TO DO IT YOURSELF!
?
THE EVIL QUEEN WOULD NEVER DEMEAN HERSELF BY TAKING OUT THE TRASH!
??
SHORTLY AFTER...
I'VE REALLY STARTED TO WORK ON MY ROLE! IT'S FUN TO BE BAD!
YAY, JULIE!

Don't Miss DANCE CLASS #8 "Snow White and the Seven Dwarves"
Available Now at Booksellers Everywhere!